SWERVING SIZES

One-, Three-, and Two-Hundred-Word Stories

Michael Cocchiarale

Unsolicited Press
Portland, Oregon
www.unsolicitedpress.com
info@unsolicitedpress.com
619-354-8005

SWERVING SIZES
Copyright © 2026 Michael Cocchiarale
All Rights Reserved.
Printed in the United States of America.
First Edition.
ISBN: 978-1-963115-91-8

This is a work of fiction. Any resemblance to actual people, living or dead, is pure coincidence—or just your imagination running wild. If you think you see yourself in these pages, congrats, but nope… not you.

All rights are reserved. That means no part of this book may be reproduced, copied, shared, screen-grabbed, tattooed, or otherwise distributed without written permission from the publisher. Translation: don't steal our words. If you love this book, buy it, gift it, rave about it to strangers—just don't pirate it.
Now that the legal stuff is out of the way, go ahead and dive in.

Distributed by Asterism Books
https://asterismbooks.com/

For wholesale orders:
Asterism Books
568 1st Avenue South, Ste 120
Seattle, WA 98104
(206) 485-4829
info@asterismbooks.com

Cover: Kathryn Gerhardt
Editor: Summer Stewart

For restrictions, and the freedoms to which they give rise

CONTENTS

REGULAR

QUARANTINE	13
GENAU	14
THE HEIGHT OF HER POWERS	16
YELLOW TRAIL	17
LAST DAYS OF MAY	18
VIOLATORS WILL BE OWED	20
STERRETTANIA	21
BREAK ROOM, SMITTY'S ON THE LEVEE	23
THE ICE IS ALWAYS BREAKING	25
WING NIGHT	27
GAME CHANGER	28
PORTION	30
CONJUGATE	32
AN UNFINISHED PRAYER	33
NO NEWS	34
THE WARDROBE	36
DEPRESSION	38
GARBAGE TIME	39
THEY WILL LET HIM KNOW	41
VARIABLES	43
A PROBLEM KEY	44

MISFIT	46
MORE A NOTHING THAN A SOMETHING	47
WE SHOULD GO	49
BULL'S EYE IS A SIGN	50
FIRST CLEAR MORNING OF A WEEK AT ST. IVES	52
STIMULUS CHECK	53
BACK UP	55
KIMBERLY MAYBE	56
AUGUST AFTERNOON, DELAWARE COUNTY, PA	58
THE EXTREMELY ARDENT ACTIVIST	59
LONG LIGHT	61
LAST DANCE	63
THE CHILD THAT'S THAT	64
THE ANGEL OF DEATH VICTORIOUS	66

EXTRA

WAY TO GO	71
THE ARC OF THE MORAL UNIVERSE	72
THE FATHER WHO NEVER KNEW WHEN	73
FIRST SESSION OF THE LAST FULL DAY OF THE LONELINESS SYMPOSIUM	76
MEME AND RESPONSE	77
HOW MANY WERE THERE?	79

CREDIT CARD SONG	81
DEAR CROSSING	82
THE GALLERY OF NEARLY EMPTY ROOMS	84
SIGNALS	86
A PARABLE FOR YOU KNOW WHO	88
BALL DROP	89
SOCIETY RESPONDS HAPHAZARDLY TO ACCUSATIONS OF DYSTOPIA	91
THE CITY OF MY BIRTH	92
LISTENAMERICA: AN EPIC FIVE-PART MINI-SERIES	93
WE OPENED AND WE OPENED AND WE GORGED TO SAVE OUR LIVES	100
MIRACLE WORKER	101
ROUND AND ROUND WE GO	103
PRETTY LITTLE LAWN	104
UNDER REVIEW	105
PASTWORD RESET	107
SANCTUARY CITY	108
RESPONSES TO THE CHARGE THAT HISTORY WILL NOT BE KIND	110
MONSTERS KEEP COMING	111
BAD TIMING	113
BAD APPLES	115
WRONG SIDE OF HISTORY	117

GRANDMA BREEN GETS CHRISTMAS MEAN	119
SERVING SUGGESTIONS	121
SCALING THE NORTH FACE OF STUPIDITY	123
THE DAY THAT'S COMING FOR YOU	125
NOT AS EASY AS IT SOUNDS	127
STRIKING	129
WANTHOLES	130
WHAT A JOKE	132
WANTED	133
A DISVERBING PROCEDURE	135
TRUE STORY	137
BIG THIRD THING	139
IN THE END, AREN'T EPIPHANIES THE BEST?	141

SWERVING SIZES

REGULAR

QUARANTINE

When watching windows grew old, they tried many new things: recipes, languages, positions. One morning, a friend texted, "soap cutting videos!" After breakfast, they took laptop and bottle to bed. He clicked play, and they watched the blade slide, soap pebbles like cereal spilling down in its wake. Occasionally, they sipped champagne. Neither said a word.

After, she sighed, "Another?" He stared at blinds; she felt across his body for play. He wanted to say there was tomorrow, the next and the next. They should spread out the fun, a pat of butter over a long dark slice of toast.

GENAU

As the train approached, my wife's high-spirited boss started in about the summer of seventy-something, her coming-of-age excursion to Gay Paris. In the Alps, this pony-tailed lass was struggling with luggage down the aisle. When she stopped to gather herself, her phrase book dropped into our storyteller's lap. Near tears, the girl asked in awkward German, "Is this seat taken?"

My wife cried, "How sweet," smiling as she often did for others.

Frau Boss and her "partner" had invited us for Mittagessen—a spread of meats and cheese, with local pilsner no better than beer in the States. After, in stingy sun, this woman sat with our daughter on a blanket, explaining a book of romantic landscapes. Elated, my wife snapped several shots.

The train hissed, but Frau Boss was nowhere near her happy ending. "One more," my wife said, waving her and our daughter together for a photo before a cloying backdrop of canola.

Seated, fuming, I watched the train station's sign pass by. Black and white against brick the color of dried blood. The town's umlaut glared.

I asked, "You get your fill?"

Under-the-breath bickering ensued, our daughter a barbed wall between us. Finally, fed up, my wife turned to hone her Deutsch with a handsome woman across the aisle.

*

Years later, my daughter called: "Remember Frau Müller?"

"You mean that—"

"Stop. She died."

I nodded at nobody. "And I'm supposed to feel—?"

"Ja," she drawled. "Genau."

"What? Speak English."

She answered—bitch—with a sudden click.

Now the woman I'd married wasn't dead, just blissfully far away. Online—over the years—I've shared few hard feelings. And, in my further defense, didn't I just yesterday 'like' a picture of her with my replacement, cavorting on one of those islands so pleased to have her kind?

THE HEIGHT OF HER POWERS

Mom, yeah, remember her? Less and less, I know. I ever tell you, years back, two weeks before she off—or, excuse me, "*before her untimely passing*"—I asked what she thought her best self was, you know, at the height of her powers. She looked up from her crossword puzzle, as if the answer was flashing in front of her eyes, and said, "I was twenty-seven." I don't remember much more, except that it was the one and only honest conversation we ever had.

I bet she said twenty-seven because of that roofer—the hunky guy on Dad's softball team. You were two, a saggy diaper always crying to be picked up, but I was old enough to notice things. I remember sitting on the porch steps one summer evening, eyes moving between my Superman comic and this unbuttoned Adonis who yapped Yanks and Sox with Dad. A cocktail—something blue—rested on Mom's knee while her bare toes kept slow pitching out toward the guy again and again, only to fall back lonely through the air. All that distance, that air. I can't wrap my brain around it. Does no good to hate her for it. I guess.

YELLOW TRAIL

At seven miles, Red struck Vic as the road to certain death. Yellow, at one point three, seemed the safer choice. Clearer too, with stiff boards over intermittent muck.

Halfway, by stone ruins, a sallow man stood, green gloves snapping branches.

"Steve?"

It was—Ridley letterman, dead eye off the bench. Since then: drugs, divorce, DWIs. Last week, he'd been taken in.

"Scam?"

"*Taken in*—for questioning. About that Middletown Bludgeoneer."

Vic stepped back, slipping from plank into mud.

"Ha—you don't think . . ."

He could only plead, "Fresh air."

Steve gleamed. "Right? Sometimes, don't you feel lucky to be alive?"

LAST DAYS OF MAY

After my last exam, I stopped to see my brother, who'd just invented a holiday that required him to call off work.

"Eponymas?" I said.

"The holy day of self-titled debut albums!"

I sat, enveloped by the smell of marijuana and whatever it was that wafted from his work-friend Mab, who brooded inside a hoodie on the cat-killed couch.

"Today," my brother said, "it's BOC."

When I named my favorite song, Mab ahhed his appreciation. The smell reminded me of roadside decay.

"Seriously? 'Burning for You?'" My brother palmed off his bandana and shook out lawless hair. "Buck the popular opinions.'" He slid the disc into his hand. "The early stuff's what's real. When a band's still faithful to themselves."

He dropped the needle. Crack and fizz. Then came the clear, austere lead.

"First verse," my brother said. "Story's all there. Naïve dudes, desert landscape, cash for dope, the hint of inevitable betrayal." He glanced at Mab. "That right?"

While listening, I studied the curtains—a tattered flag with the words "NO SURRENDER" slapped across red and black.

Mab drew the strings of his hoodie before offering me a joint. When I shook my head, he said, "Your loss," the room blooming again with that corpse-like smell.

"No—his *gain*." My brother squeezed my shoulder. "He's not going to go along with the crowd."

The boys were now dead, the song nearly done. Eyes flickering, my brother stood to twist the lock on the door. "Trust, faith," he said. "All's well and good until someone loses a life."

Mab passed his stink with the joint. My brother inhaled and held his breath, eyes fixed on the shadow beneath the hood. At the end of the month, hauled in by his boss for theft, he'd let it all out for good.

VIOLATORS WILL BE OWED

Bloody Marys at the old haunt uptown, and now, still two hours from home, she's made them stop so she can press a hand against the glass of the dorm where she'd lived five years ago.

"We probably shouldn't." He glances back at the car, parked where it doesn't belong.

She moves to the door to try it. "Hey—Memory Lane!"

He blinks; she's gone.

One night—sophomore year—he'd driven up, her roommate out of town. She laid out crackers, cheese, talked about God knew what. He closed his eyes. Downed beer. Finally, he saw an opening and went to work. Kissed lips and neck, crawled under the shirt, dragged off sweats. There'd been squirming. Had she even said a word?

Next morning, Mom shook him up for his shift. He held his head, tongued cotton in his mouth. Ghost-like, the night before returned—her quiet tears, the awkward cleaning up. He'd felt pretty bad. Still, in the years since, she hadn't seemed to hold much against him.

The sign has been vandalized, but he can still make out the fees and where they take offenders. It's summer, though, and the campus is dead. Could the penalties still apply?

STERRETTANIA

What a land! the boy thought, conjuring pictures of rough-hewn cottages, cobblestone lanes, wizards and knights, maidens with golden hair.

"Can we stop?" he asked, the green sign approaching.

Mom turned, smiling brightly. Dad said, "If we stopped everywhere, we'd get nowhere at all."

The exit slipped by. He turned, straining against the belt for a glimpse. Was the village behind that Jesus billboard? Beyond the mom and pop motels? For miles after, this magical past-place remained an orb of fire in his heart.

Next morning, in another country, he sulked in a raincoat through cramped caves under the falls, lost in thought about his Sterrettania. He saw himself tying up his horse, ducking through a doorway that led into an inn, cradling a mug of mead while some wizened herbalist proffered wares before a fire. Later, the innkeeper's daughter, guiding him with a candle to his room, asked, "Have you come to seek the elixir of youth?"

Hands like irons clasped his own. "Come to the edge," Dad said, grinning beneath his hood.

"Honey, don't," Mom said. "He's scared."

Too late: He was at the opening, water a hard white roar before him. He couldn't help but see townsfolk fleeing, stumbling, angry waves like scythes slicing everyone down before they could reach higher ground.

He imagined centuries from now, archeologists unearthing artifacts: a vase, a wooden doll, a leather-bound journal kept by the daughter in that inn. Page one, a single line: "Tomorwe, my lyf with thee bygynneth."

"Son—Jesus—stop crying!"

In social studies last week, they'd watched this documentary that showed human bones in an ancient Roman crypt. The narrator's voice was stern. Biblical. He could hear it now, bursting through the roar: "As you are, we once were. As we are, you shall be one day."

BREAK ROOM, SMITTY'S ON THE LEVEE

"There oughta be a rule," Angelica said, jabbing a shoe into the space between his boots. "At least three steps for a dance."

"You can't even . . ." He touched her shoulders, showed her where to put hands before moving her—one-two, one-two. She studied his eyes. He couldn't believe how little there was between them. "Quick-quick," he said. "Slow-slow."

Last week, on his way from break back to Dairy, he'd noticed her in Meats. The next day, she grinned crazily behind the glass, raising a cleaver for effect.

"Maybe—"

"Follow my lead."

Yesterday evening, sent to the lot for carts, he gawked at a parade of tight jeans and ten gallons striding toward the Cactus Club next door. Ridiculous or cool? Maybe they could scoot their way into the spree in between?

"You smell like a baby."

"Huh?"

"Milk."

Her bloody apron spoiled the picture he'd conjured of them dressed to the cowpoke nines.

She grinned. "One-two percent."

Hurt, he stuck thumbs into belt loops. He pantomimed a cheek with chaw.

"But you've got a few moves," Angelica said, slugging his arm. "I'll give you that."

One-two—such stupid simple math. But she, though sharp, would never add them up.

THE ICE IS ALWAYS BREAKING

My father—eighty-two—has never been known for metaphor. No, directness is his club of choice. For example:
- "Shut up."
- "Be a man."
- "I'm moving. You've got three days to grab your stuff."

Among the thick plastic shrouds in the attic, I come across a shaky pyramid of toys. I pick one up, and the mildewed box gives way, chunks of white plastic chattering on the floor.

"The ice game," I say.

"You couldn't stand it."

He tips two trunks and insists we sit and play. As he inserts cubes into the frame, I think about last week's phone message: "Son, I'm lying in my own damn blood." I rushed to the house, found him at the bottom of the stairs, red running down his face. The morning after the night in the emergency room, I returned to clean things up.

"You could have died!" I said, stirring crystals into hot water from the tap.

He shrugged. "What doesn't kill me will try again later."

Dad inserts the plastic man in the center square. I palm away sweat that had dropped in my eye.

"Nervous," he says—not a question but a charge.

He hands me a mallet, and we take turns tapping one cube after another to the floor below. Soon, the plastic man is nearly surrounded by open space. Dad glances from one side of the frame to the other. The mallet hovers.

"Are you okay?"

"There was another one you liked. One of those old game shows? *Password*? *Joker's Wild*?" Dad runs a finger thoughtfully over his scar. "Maybe *Jeopardy*."

"Is that your final answer?"

His swing brings the plastic man down.

"I forget, was there ever a show for *Life*?"

Dad smiles. "That's the one where contestants sat on their asses, dumb about what was coming."

WING NIGHT

Nearby, a woman points above her guy. "How many again for a score?"

"That's cute," Tom smiles, pinching a wing.

Beer-battered Bill barks, "Handsome!"

Drew frowns. "Hmm, pretty poor choice of—"

"For her? C'mon." Bill aspires to stand, but his ass is having none of it.

John adjusts his frames. "Handsome, the origin of it—"

"Winsome?" says Tom.

"Losesome!" Bill brays, spiking bones into basket.

Drew winces. "Boyfriend's hearing you."

On the screen, a linebacker lays out the player who made the pass.

"It simply meant 'easy to maneuver,'" John says.

Bill belches. "Even so. Who'd want to?"

GAME CHANGER

"Wait—Katie's getting dunked *next week?*"

Classic Aaron, Steve thinks. Hardly a thing he won't try to trivialize.

Mark says, "Lisa didn't tell you?"

"My two cents: You best wait until winter. At least Father D. won't be sweating so damn much."

Mark grimaces. "Do not make me disinvite you to the baptism."

"Come on. You ever shake his hand? See how he mops his head? And that creeper smile?" Aaron looks to Steve and Dean for help. He thrives on a good gang up, when he can get one. "It all adds up to pedo priest."

"Sometimes," Mark says, "sometimes you don't know when—"

"Hey, guys, I, I've got to tell you," Dean says, his eyes already regretting it.

"Yes, we know," Aaron says. "It's obvious, and there's absolutely nothing to be ashamed—"

"I have cancer."

"Jesus," Mark says, steadying the beer he's nearly spilled.

Dean digs behind an ear. "Never mind. They caught it early."

"I'm really sorry."

"Nah, I just thought you—" He waves a hand. "Docs are on the job. Sorry, I—"

"Which kind?" Aaron again, his tone hard to figure.

"Prostate. Early. Forget it." He lifts his pint. "We're drinking beer!"

Aaron belches, and Mark skids his chair back with a glare.

Standing, Dean says, "I think I'll hit the head."

Aaron shrugs. "Hey, when you gotta go . . ."

Mark's eyes flash like fists at Aaron's flippant jaw. Steve sighs, shrinks, seeks refuge in where they all began: those grade school days, that runner-up year. Pizza parties, locker room pranks, layup lines, hands in a circle before the whistle was blown. And, of course, that championship game: halftime, ahead by a cool dozen, lined up to lean lips toward the pure jump shot of fountain water that always appeared when they pressed.

PORTION

Dad could not get enough of Rosie, the easy-going nutritionist who, following a filling picnic at the lake, squeezed our shoulders and said, "Mom wants to cook for you two."

After a recent scare, Dad had transformed himself into a health food nut. He cooked with measuring cups. "Ten portions of fruits and vegetables a day!" he'd say when I turned my nose up at the raw pepper slices grinning on my plate. He knew what he was in for with Rosie's Mom; still, he said, "Sure!"

*

Dad said, "A serving size of pasta is one ounce."

Rosie's mother tonged a steaming pile of noodles onto his plate. "Questa è un'oncia!"

We laughed. Dad, nodded, took a breath, and started twirling. When he pushed the empty plate away, Rosie, clasping her hands, said, "My hero!" He leaned into her arms. Rosie's mother smiled, waving a fork back and forth. "You two, I like."

'Like' left me wanting. I was head-over-heels *in love*.

*

Rosie's mom thumbed the bible, finding what she wanted. Psalms: "My flesh and my heart may fail, but God is the strength of my heart and my portion forever."

Dad said, "Food for the soul!"

Rosie rolling eyes was a present all for me.

*

We were stabbing salads by the river when Dad broke the news.

Through tears, I tried to make things light. "It was all that pasta, right?"

His smile was distracted, obligatory. "Sometimes, well, we just figure out what's not good for us."

"But you're crazy about her!" I remembered Rosie's smile, her hand on mine, the way she soothed adolescent pains with tender eyes. Emptiness consumed me—worse than when I'd watched my mother go.

Dad opened his mouth. I waited, but he just sat still, dead-eyed, making a steady diet of the breeze.

CONJUGATE

Mother was failing French on the front porch swing. Hurried, hard, I spared just seconds to lecture: "Désirer—regular verb. Voler. Détester. Conjugation's the same."

"Merci," she whispered, wincing at the time. There was laundry left, an experiment with cassoulet.

That night in the dollar store lot, some jeune fille helped me off into her hands. Back home, trashed, I popped the can to find meat drunk in an ooze of fat.

Mother never finished the course. The degree. Today, I was told she'd died alone. Mourir, I recalled—one of those heartless irregulars.

I hardly knew where to begin.

AN UNFINISHED PRAYER

The pages of the bible chattered in the wind. After much flipping, June read at random, words far above me like a plane with a sign at a beachfront resort. She tried to light a candle, but the flame wouldn't catch. While she sang, his picture from the war slid to the ground. No matter. She went on, my snazzy sis, who flew in so we could say there'd been a crowd. I was the one who'd never get away. Screwed early, I'd left the bawling result with a sitter for the day.

After, June sprang for burgers before returning home. "Work tomorrow," she said, zipping up her leather jacket.

I had time, so I went back for one more shot at closure. First, I brushed my hand across the casket, trying—I don't know—to wipe away the times I wished him dead. I knocked on wood, waited like a fool for an apology. Finally, on my knees, I let loose: "Our father, who loved us rarely, hollow was thy goddamn heart." Bitter lines—they thrilled me until they didn't. Desperate, I added "Still" but the word took off, a delicate winged thing with no future need to land.

NO NEWS

Dannie calls and she never calls, so you know the news is bad. Thing is, you've just made this killer lunch. As it steams on the front porch table, you're thinking it may well be the single best stir fry of your life.

But there's the phone call. The message had said, "Trace, hi, I, well, it's been. But I have. I have some news so, anyway, when you get the chance." The voice broke. There'd definitely been tears.

You eat, the scenarios gnawing at your mind. Dannie's mother had been ill. A lung thing. Cancer? Her brother—what was his name?—owed thousands before heading for the hills.

You eat more quickly, trying hard to relish crunch and tang. Maybe something with Dannie? An accident? A grim diagnosis?

You nod at the masked mailperson gagging the slot with circulars. You're a careful, responsible sort—always have been. But why had you brought this woman upon yourself? Had it been love? Or were you only starved for sex that might finally give a fuck? What if (you wince) it was simply because your decadent self-loathing was way too much for one?

You are full. On the plate, a few grains of rice drowse in a sensual whoosh of sauce. The neighborhood is quiet. The crone next door has hauled in her rambunctious grandkids for a snack. A few doors down, landscapers have finished their assault on a lawn. A breeze suddenly teases. Sun drops through the screen onto your crimson toes. It's July, but people are still being told to keep their distance. Which, all things considered, is quite fine by you.

What next? Tea. Yes—peppermint iced tea. Back on the porch, you sigh, turning full attention to the cheerful report of the birds that flutter about the feeder.

THE WARDROBE

I'm sipping coffee at a bar in Schöneberg when this man appears across from me. Swigging his Kindl, he tells me he's in Berlin for the year.

"Such history," I say.

"You a tourist?" He tips his beer toward memorabilia behind me.

"I'm looking for a new start."

"You and the world. You know Bowie, though?"

"'Changes?'"

"If that's the best you can do. In the 70s, this here was his favorite bar."

I say I'd just wanted a place to rest.

"He's coming back, you know."

"Who?"

"Bowie!"

"Isn't he—?"

"Listen, mate." He scrapes his chair toward mine. "I bought that wardrobe at an auction. The one from 'Lazarus.' Last video he made."

I remember.

"Someday, he'll step back out, dressed in some slick new skin. Not Ziggy, not the Thin White Duke."

When the coffin closed, I forgot my mother's face.

"I'll be front row for something never seen."

As a teen, attempting to come close, I'd sneak into her closet, slip into dresses and precipitous heels, items she'd saved for occasions that never came. Now, those clothes are gone forever. At Goodwill, some spaced-out guy shrugged and said, "Guess you can toss 'em on that heap."

DEPRESSION

There's that shirt, the sky blue one, bought by his wife because she said it'd look nice on him, pinned and stiff on the window seat, six feet from the bed. He pushes back the sheet. Twitches a leg. Attempts to imagine what it'll take to reach this shirt and try it on. To check sleeve length. To cut the tag and bring it down to wash. To climb the stairs and put it on again. To button every button. To tuck it in. To venture down once more. To speak. To open the door for all that fucking sun.

GARBAGE TIME

Midway through the fourth, fifty-six to zip, and yet another doomed play—this one, a blast up the middle into an immovable mass. Whistles. Fraught disentanglements. The team's running back writhes on the turf.

Another break. Dead space on the screen. I say, "Well, they've covered—"

"The spread," Dad says, catching the pass I tossed.

A commercial: toothsome teens gushing about fantastic cell phone plans.

Now what? I could use the bathroom, but I'd done that during the time out a minute before. Another bourbon? Not food—Mom and Dana are picking up steaks. There's always weather, unseasonable for November.

Dad says, "In the end, we lose it all."

I hide surprise with a sigh. "Not life everlasting. Don't you listen at church?"

"Ever do something just to please somebody?"

This, I nearly say. This moribund attempt at bonding.

"I'm angry. Spitting nails. And when I'm dead, I'll lose even that."

Last week, Mom had called to say something about tests. Dad leans toward me now. "Meta, metas," he whispers. "Anyway, it's game over."

On TV, a woman sniffs a room that could use a wipe and spray.

"Your mother doesn't . . ."

I just can't. I stand, shake my head, walk around the end table to the kitchen, where a white bag ghosts the left-open can. Grounds like topsoil, eggshells from the morning. I tie and run the trash into the early evening emptiness. The maple's weeping leaves. A red ball gags the foul mouth of the sewer.

Back inside, Dad's eyes are sealed. On the screen, a third-string wideout soars across the end zone until his shoulders drop as if shot. The camera pans to a yellow flag and arms over a striped shirt's head. The play is coming back. It never really happened is what those whistles meant.

THEY WILL LET HIM KNOW

Sleek corridors, the windows long gone. Around a corner, a cool inhuman room. To the right of the bed, cylindrical containers, a vial of clear liquid, a long syringe.

"Relax," the doctor says. "There will be more pressure than pain."

And there is—a positive sign, or maybe something close.

His cells are bottled, sealed, and labeled for a lab in an adjacent state. He imagines them the next day shuddering on a shelf inside a crowded fridge, the ominous thrum of tires against pavement below. "Where are we going?" they cry aloud. "What on earth could be wrong?"

At the parking kiosk, he decides to ask for help.

"You ready for the holidays?" the attendant wonders, inserting his card, plopping buttons with a fist.

"No."

"Tell me about it."

It's tempting, but hasn't he surrendered enough of himself for one day?

"Would you like a receipt?"

"No. But thank you."

The attendant smiles. "Then you're good to go!"

He wanders in darkness until he finds his car. At the exit, pursed lips swallow the parking card like a pill. The gate rises, and he crawls into the sunny December morning, which will last precisely as long as it's able.

VARIABLES

A fraction of a second after he passed her, he braked to one-eighty. She'd already stopped, eyes sharpening to points. If she hadn't been wearing a mask, might he have seen the arc of a smile?

"Wow," she said. "It's been . . . how long?"

"I defer to the math wiz."

"It's a matter of simple subtraction."

He waited. For clarification? Correction? Then he tried "Are you—?" before stopping, the ways he might finish multiplying in his mind.

She put hands on her hips. He had too. A month ago, they'd run their hands all over. Now, there was only small talk, masked. He could feel her measuring their distance.

"Weren't," she said. "Why are you back?"

He shrugged, fingering his chin strap. "Full circle?"

A child suddenly divided them. "What about me?" he cried, sliding down to friends by the creek. Yesterday, there'd been heavy rain. Today, the Brandywine ran brown.

"Well, it's been . . ." She glanced at the asphalt beyond.

"Wait." He squeezed handle grips. "You, we, we can try to solve—"

"Matt." She dropped her mask. "No do-overs."

The taut slope of bloodless lips only reinforced her points: he was her ex—and doubtless her why as well.

A PROBLEM KEY

"Am I right?" the attendant asked.

Embarrassed, Evan parked chin upon clavicle.

"I tried for ten minutes!" The attendant forced him to see thumb and forefinger. "I was *this close* to towing."

An old woman in line pursed her lips. A teen flicked peevishly at her phone.

"Let's go."

Evan approached the elevator. There was a car inside—a silver BMW.

"Get in. Move up, move up. Stay there."

The door dropped, and the elevator rose. "This one," he said, slapping the hood of the vehicle, "you put in the key, it starts right away."

The door opened.

"Move back."

The attendant climbed into the BMW and roared it into a nearby spot. He beckoned, and Evan followed to his own drab Corolla. The attendant got in and aimed his angry face out the open window. "There. You see I'm turning it. Nothing happens. Ten minutes!"

Evan said, "The thing is, the key's bent. You've got to push it up a bit."

The attendant tried twice more before it started. "You can't park in Philadelphia. Not this car. You know what I put up with?"

He squealed into the elevator. Together, they descended in silence. The door opened, and the attendant gunned the Corolla out to the street. The people in line watched, heartless pleasure in their eyes.

Evan paid. Receipt in hand, he began to tear. "I'm sorry."

The attendant barked, "Next customer."

He left, steering aimlessly down one-way streets. Home was an option, but hadn't he enough rancor for the night? Later, a left brought him by the garage again, where the attendant sat smoking on an overturned bucket. Impulsively, Evan waved. After a moment, the man lifted a hand. Stood up to peer. Evan braked and watched the mirror, longing for even a slight swerve of smile.

MISFIT

Second Father gobbled sausage like First glugged gin. "Anyway, I'm sorry," he said, his fork and knife through ground-up flesh.

The misfit risked a glance. Tissues bloomed like upside-down daisies from the broad holes of the fat man's nose.

"When I bleed," he said, "That's when you've got to believe what I'm saying."

With great care, the misfit brought a last spoon of dry Os to his mouth.

"I'll tell you this: you can't lie blood."

Finished, the misfit asked to please be excused. He washed his bowl and dried it. He placed it back precisely where it belonged.

In the living room stood the artificial tree, a sick green rocket on a shoe box launching pad. Mom had still not come down to bend the branches, but the manger scene had been arranged. There were Mary, Joseph, and a one-armed savior in the straw. The misfit probed the teeth where Second Father had slugged him. Sore as usual but nothing loose.

Year after year, this holy family returned. What had they done to deserve such a fate? And why, why, during a single silent night, had they never once tried to blast off for even some slightly better star?

MORE A NOTHING THAN A SOMETHING

Joplin locks, jeans chopped off, legs pale light speeding out from Birkenstocks. That was Ray, an 8x10 now beside Dad's mantel clock. Years ago, he'd been one of the CB friends who was almost always over. Beer and bourbon bashes, Cribbage and Ouija boards, guitar-strapped drunks laying waste to Bob and Baez. The last time, I crept downstairs and found Ray shatter-eyed in the den, sliding vinyl from a sleeve.

"You know Floyd?"

I shrugged.

"They're far out," he said, Lotus style on the braided rug, head afloat upon eerie sounds emerging. "Far as possible, without going over."

In the kitchen, Dad loudly deplored the draft.

Ray said, "You were nothing for billions of years. One day, you'll be nothing evermore."

"You're something else," said Mom, appearing in the archway, tugging her miniskirt.

He winked. "Set the controls for the heart of the sun."

*

Wednesday, Ray stopped by, hair tailed, suit and tie, clutching walkie-talkies.

"Aren't you handsome," Mom said.

"Interview. My last chance."

After shooing me upstairs, Ray said, "Breaker, breaker 1-9."

"10-4, good buddy!" I exclaimed.

"Hold on. Gumballs in the rearview. Hammer down!"

From the landing, I spied Mom, her head like a capsule on the surface of Ray's shoulder.

*

The following night, I answered the phone to a woman sobbing about her Raymond, whose cycle swerved past one truck right into another. Mom appeared, saving the receiver before it struck the linoleum.

Hours after, Dad cracked my door. "Your mother's crushed."

Ray had been. A real something.

"Want the light off?"

Eyes closed, I spun the dials of my imagination. Pictured the swerve, the glare, the smash. The nothing.

"Son?"

Nothing. Nothing. Nothing. Discrete they were, like invisible sheep—one after another, up and over, colliding with more nothing on the dark side of the room.

WE SHOULD GO

For their first anniversary, they decided to cross the river for steaks. Since it was hot, they cut through the student union, stopping cold in the lobby before a crowd gathered by the monstrous TV. A quarter mile away, a story was developing. Police cars, a chopper. They watched the camera creep across the front of the dorm where the culprit was holing up. A SWAT team rolled in. Sharpshooters crouched on the rec center roof. On a couch up front sat a guy in a turned-around cap, feet up on a table, face full of meatball sub. Two girls appeared behind them, brooding over a preempted soap.

"We should go," he said.

She tugged his sleeve. "Wait, let's see how this ends."

*

After, they stopped to draw money. He slid his card into machine while she brightened lips in the window of an SUV. The deck-shuffling sound began. Then the beeping, a sign of action required. Had it been only twenty minutes since the young man turned the shotgun on himself? As he folded bills, his wife said, "I'm starved!" Nodding, following in her fragrant wake, he tried to understand how exactly his life would never be the same.

BULL'S EYE IS A SIGN

They'd recently moved to this Indiana town, with a square that was quaint until the evening they saw a Klansman standing on the courthouse stairs, hood off, chin raised for the camera's blinding white.

Win's hand fell from the one she'd been holding. It took her a moment to remember—yes, that wisp of beard, David, her husband of three weeks. He looked now like a younger version of himself after nearly slipping off a cliff. She probably didn't look much better.

"Isn't this your field?" David said, a smile trickling.

She'd just started graduate work in entomology—pest management, with a focus on ticks. She said, "I've never . . . you know, it's not funny."

There was a patrol car by the curb, an officer with crossed arms leaning up against it. Win heard voices. Laughter—it was unclear from whom.

The flashes continued, each a shock to her system. When she looked back, David was gone. No—he was under the streetlight at the door of the coffee shop, waving for her to come.

Her head brushed the branches of a tree. She winced and rushed fingers through her hair. Again came the laughter, a kind of snap like the action of the flag above them. As she approached the shop, she thought about ticks—their hunger, their poison, their sneaky insidiousness. Her favorite aunt, an avid gardener, had the disease: nerve pain, numbness, heart issues, palsy.

"That's a wrap," said a low voice from the courthouse stairs.

"Right, see you and the guys tomorrow."

"Good times," said the officer, eyes firing her way.

Win stared. She scratched a searing beneath her breasts. At the door, she moved past the hand and went inside. Track lights, scones, French roast, Sting—anything now to spare her from her husband's easy eyes.

FIRST CLEAR MORNING OF A WEEK AT ST. IVES

The son sat on the balcony, shooing flies from eggs while waves moved like promises made then unremembered. It was worse when the woman appeared, her wrap wailing in the breeze as she shoved a pram through recalcitrant sand.

He sought escape through sliding doors but slammed into a morning from years ago, his mother saying, "Once, I'd love to stay at an ocean resort. One with those breakfast buffets—made-to-order omelets, stuffed French toast." She looked up from a hard roll and jam, dropping the dream to watch a bug touring the globe that contained her dim kitchen light.

STIMULUS CHECK

What Nick was doing was quite difficult. Unprecedented. He breathed deeply, clicked "Start." This time, no do-overs, no centering of pins, no magic bomb ball that left only smoke and shards in the pit. Without help of any kind, he was going to bowl his first 300.

He ran his finger up the mouse, and the ball shot down the lane, between the second and third arrow. BAM!—a perfect strike.

Again: ten more pins in the pit.

The door squeaked, and he thought "shit" upon seeing Pawze wander in. And for what? To sniff socks on the floor? You'd think even a cat could find something better to do with his time.

Nick turned back to the screen. Ran his teeth back and forth and let the ball fly. BAM! Damn—a turkey!

Pawze leapt on the bed and fell on its side, head rubbing against Nick's toes. He drew back and rolled. Again, the pins disappeared. Christ—a four-bagger! He breathed out. Rubbed his hands against his jeans.

"Nick!" Anya was clomping upstairs. There was a thump on the wall against which he leaned. Who was in the bathroom? Leo? Lily?

"Where are the car keys?" Anya popped in. "Oh Pawzey, how are you, love?" She sat hard on the bed and stroked the cat.

The fifth ball waited. This time, he missed his mark. The ball struck the other side of the headpin, but still they all went down. A Brooklyn. Still perfect!

"Do you know—?"

"Somewhere," he waved. "Downstairs."

The toilet flushed. "Daddy!"—it was Lily, which meant trouble.

"Pawzey, show me your belly."

"I'm busy. Everyone, shut up!"

Anya stood, eyes retreating. In the hallway, Leo yelled "Loser," and Lily began to wail. Nick, taking aim, rolled his next ball straight into the gutter.

BACK UP

Grace appeared to him in flashes: sprinkling the tomatoes, chalking a driveway heart, spooning water ice on a boardwalk bench. And that one in front of the pizza place. She was maybe two, wearing a pink sunhat, crinkling the nose she'd skinned the day before by the swings. Those images and hundreds more were gone. He rebooted several times, seething at the endless spin. Finally, he heaved the laptop down the stairs.

"Real mature," Leslie said, wiping hands below. "A stunning portrait of—"

"Shut up."

"Or what?"

He stomped down the stairs and kicked the computer in its stupid cracked-up face.

"You'll break something else? Me?"

"Seriously? Get a fucking grip!"

"Lord, the irony."

He turned to see her face presenting the latest in a long series of glares. "Do you realize what we've—"

"Lost? Ha! You can't lose what you never had."

He slammed out the door, desperate to keep ahead of all he'd forgotten to save another way. At the curb, he looked back to see his daughter hovering above, framed by thick bedroom panes. He shuttered and clicked his eyes but was hardly surprised to see that this picture had vanished like all the rest.

KIMBERLY MAYBE

The child of my brother's ex came with us to the park that afternoon for what I'd known even then would be the last gasp of her childhood. We picked up subs, nothing special, and the girl (Kimberly—maybe?) was young enough to enjoy helping Melody make a gnome house between the gnarled roots of an oak.

"But where are the gnomes?" she asked.

"Well, let's see." Melody scanned the park. "Want to have a look?" She taught fourth grade and was great about giving kids another world for a while.

The girl smiled, and they hand-in-handed downhill to the woods.

"She's a real delight," I said.

My brother shrugged. "Give Tiff time. She'll turn the girl into trash."

As I took a drink of diet soda, I thought about how our family was like a car over a guardrail, head first into a pond. A frantic struggle. Screaming. I escaped through a window, desperately stroked to the surface. On occasion, I'd look back to see my brother flailing, body pinned by his belt, hair spiraling from his head. God knew where our parents had gone.

My wife returned, one hand over the other. The girl—what's her name?—danced with abandon. "We found one!" she sang.

"Careful now, gnomes are a dying breed," Melody said, placing a handful of nothing inside the home they'd made.

*

After Thanksgiving, while cleaning the credenza, I discovered a porcelain figurine with a note in Melody's hand: "For Kimberly(?), for the holidays." I turned the piece in my hand, struck by the delicate magic wand. There was a crystal orb on top, which I took to rubbing like a lamp. Then, inspired, I thumbed it back until it snapped. There—it looked better now, a stupid stick, which was much more true to life.

AUGUST AFTERNOON, DELAWARE COUNTY, PA

Strollers and bikes cruise along the paved path that flows around the memorial park. In the pavilion, three middle-aged men in ghostly tees sweat to bring oldies back to life. "My Girl" first, then the off-key "ooohs" of "She's Gone." Outside the park, beyond the refreshment stand, a blacktop lane slides toward the side door of a funeral home, from which a casket is descending. Plodding Hall & Oates rocks the pine boat steered by pallbearers into the dark shell of the hearse. Next door, oblivious to the mourners, customers pour from WAWA, toting coffee and hoagies for the road.

THE EXTREMELY ARDENT ACTIVIST

The boy pretends to head into the bank. Instead, crouching by his bumper, he turns his phone on the fools holding signs by the intersection. Slipping back into his seat, he drives toward the exit. He lives south of the strip mall but takes a right instead, inspired by an even better way to own them. Steering with a knee, he records his middle finger over the protesters along the road. That's when he sees Kaylee, bobbing a sign that says *LOVE!* He loses himself in her smile, those fingers clutching the rosy cleavage of a heart.

The car strikes then straddles the curb. When he jerks the wheel back, there's a scrape and thunk. Oh God, the boy thinks, pounding the wheel. If there's damage, Dad will have his head. At the light, he checks underneath and believes everything's fine. Back at the mall, they're still at it. Like they hadn't even seen what he'd done.

In his room, the boy posts the video along with the comment, "White guilt matters!" On the toilet seat, dreaming of Kaylee, he beats furiously until he bursts. Back at his laptop, he's crushed to see only a single like. To be fair, the afternoon is gorgeous. Snit's busy flipping burgers, and Flake's at that Boy Scout thing. In time, numbers would rise.

Later, his big brother watches, shaking smoked almonds from a bag. 'Lordy," he says. "That all you got?"

"Bet this goes viral."

"You didn't get in their faces?" He crunches nuts. "Break some shit?"

The boy signs "No" with a shrug.

Laughing, his brother farts his way out the door.

The boy refreshes, but there's still nothing new. He shifts in his stiff-backed chair. While waiting for interest to grow, he reaches down to unstick tender skin from soiled underwear.

LONG LIGHT

Yoga, juice bar, farmers market. A fine day, more or less, until Lise braked for the light at Edgemont. First in line, she found herself facing Buried Treasures, the antique store across the road. In the years since moving here, she'd tried countless times to get her mother to visit, using (among other tactics) a detailed description of the charming front porch to entice her. The ruddy sea captain, lantern swinging from outstretched hand. The cherry-red Vespa. Elegant ladies in antique cigarette signs. But Mom didn't drive. Wouldn't train or bus. Fly? "Are you kidding?" she coughed. Did Lise think she wanted to die?

Well, she was dead now. And Lise might have made it through the day without dwelling had the red not stopped her. Last week, with her awkward, soon-to-be ex, she'd ventured inside. He lumbered toward kitchenware. She closed her eyes around pedestal ashtrays to a table of postcards from a century ago. "In New York. Tomorrow we cross!" said one with an otherworldly rendering of Niagara Falls. There was another—the Liberty Bell, with its lovely scar. "Dear Mother," wrote Elaine to Mrs. Robert Archambeau of Clarion, PA. "Hard to believe: we're off to Europe!" Lise's eyes burned from these spiraling, smoky words of the dead.

The ex loomed. "For our future home," he declared, holding out a spice rack as if she were the wall on which it would hang.

"Mom had one just like it," she said. Hers, though, held only two bottles: one for salt, the other for nothing at all.

A beep from behind. Startled, Lise crawled back out of her thoughts. The light—another senseless brute—had decided to turn green at last. Longer, insistent sounds made it clear she was supposed to just step on the gas now and go.

LAST DANCE

This was how it ended: Dad wallflowered by the open door, shouting to the world he'd be leaving "ON MY OWN TURNS!" and Mom, two steps behind, hand to stomach, stopping as if shot. "Your own turns?" Her laugh became a shout. She spun and spun until falling on her knees to the hardwood floor. "Own turns?" she gasped, eyes closed, tears streaming. "*Turns*!"

Dad was dumb, fixed in place, as if he feared the slightest move would twist the whole whip-smart world down upon him, which, even now, I want to imagine he might have sometimes thought he deserved.

THE CHILD THAT'S THAT

Above, somewhere, the carol with the questions.

Mom said, "You can't possibly . . ."

"I can. *I do*."

"Words." She dumped a can of Crisco in the cart. "When people say 'love,' they mean 'endure.'"

"You don't know—"

Mom turned, hand against chest. "My whole life knows."

Growing up, I'd been taught to think of people like traffic. But from day one, Viv and I more or less cruised. After the engagement, we bought a bungalow. Immediately, we went to town, ripping out carpet, knocking down walls. New cabinets for the kitchen, pastels in the living room and den. Evenings, breathless from work and renovation, we sat wrapped in a blanket on our deck, sipping wine and planning how to make the place even more of our own. I understood when Viv sometimes said, "Please slow down!" The problem was, there was so much undoing to be done.

Mom flung food dye into the cart. "A man and a woman."

"Who?" I wasn't home to give her any satisfaction.

"After the glow, the getting used to. By the time you." She stopped on the verge of using her own poor life choice to throw shit on my own.

The loudspeaker said, "Clean up, condiments."

Mom's face hardened. I thought: coffee crystals clumping on a damp teaspoon.

"What now?" For the hell of it, I leaned on the crossbar of the cart to pop a wheelie.

"Condiments—that sounds disgusting."

I laughed, thinking of Viv's tongue inside me. The cart landed with a bang.

Mom stared as a customer rolled by. "You can be such a child."

I smiled. "Love keeps me young."

"Watch the eggs."

Her eyes said much more: "You're thirty-two" and "Stop already with all the gay."

I waited for declarations. I licked lips for another head-on Christmas crash.

THE ANGEL OF DEATH VICTORIOUS

"He's got to be a hoarder," Chaela said, finger falling from the wing of the green-tinged angel.

"He?"

She blinked. "God. You know, the *Father*?"

Gabby smiled. The church had gotten one thing right: only a man could have caused so much pain.

"How's he have room up there—for all the souls? And all the events and the memories everybody ever had."

Gabby imagined her sister's soul, dangling from a jammed drawer in a room bursting with centuries of traumatized dead. And there was the creator, splayed across a loveseat, thumbing food stains on his muscleman tee.

"God must be super sad."

She pictured a new shipment of souls spewing across the floor. "I think the whole thing just got away from him."

The angel had been crying black tears long before Gabby's mother took her and her sister to this cemetery years ago. Once, they climbed the Garfield Memorial to look at the lake. "You can't see the end of it," her mother had said. 'And this one's just the smallest of the five. Just imagine life ever after with the Lord." She smiled, stroked their heads. This was what passed for her for comfort.

"Do you think Auntie misses me?"

Gabby let that go. Nodding at the angel, she said, "Look at this sword."

"Actually, it's a torch upside down."

The deliberate snuffing of the flame. Chaela knew what Gabby wouldn't say aloud.

"Ready?" she asked.

Chaela sniffed, nodded.

At the car, Gabby felt the first damp plinks of real fear. Her sister was dead. Mom too, and Dad more or less. Already, her daughter was eight. Soon to be nine. Then ten. Past and future pained around them. She could almost see thick drops strike and glisten, before sneaking like stones into the soft, insatiable soil.

EXTRA

WAY TO GO

When notified of their impending demise, the couple deleted the forms. Who didn't in those early, incredulous days?

Undaunted, The Easement sent symptoms: fever, chills, piercing pains.

Then options. Shivering, costly meds nearly gone, the couple scrolled: Cliff, Lava, Ocean, Amber.

"Amber!" Wife croaked. "That story in the news. Two prehistoric flies, caught in 'the act' forever."

Husband laughed, his thin cage rattling. "Our final act of resistance!"

"Porno"—cough—"for posterity!"

A Finisher—polite, unassuming—came to install all the equipment. Sober now, the couple disrobed, climbed into bed.

"What you'll feel is smooth," the Finisher explained. "Close your eyes. Imagine honey."

The dispenser zoomed to a point above the bed. Husband turned, craned, saw the first drop form upon its round metallic lips. He watched it fall, felt the warm, gorgeous splash on the small of his back. They kissed. Coughed hard. When the Finisher said "Go," Husband eased inside. Wife's thin legs strained for the ceiling. The second drop landed. She whispered, "Bye." Laughing, crying, he buried his face into her neck.

"Lovely," the Finisher declared. "Hold it there." Drop three. "Wow, this is the first. On behalf of The Easement, I thank you for your service!"

THE ARC OF THE MORAL UNIVERSE

is actually a hose—bent, kinked, spun up like a snake. All you want is to undo the mess enough to stretch the nozzle towards your puny garden, where fruit is dropping dead on cracked-up earth. People shout from windows: "Lord, a gun! Police!" You plead for help. Pull, untwist, slip nozzle through endless coils. Leaks! From here and there, water shoots your face. "Justice!" roars the mob. You go under, the world a sea-mean swirl. That night, the vigil over, someone sneaks out to wrench the spigot right. After-the-fact kindness, sure, but less a solution than one final irony.

THE FATHER WHO NEVER KNEW WHEN

1979

    I'm Rumpelstiltskin, here for your first-born dinner roll!

1982

    Just a story, love. Might sit you in time out, but we'd never leave you starving in the woods.

1987

    Had you when I was young. Had your mother when I was younger. That's a pun—something just for laughs. You're old enough. Honey, is she old enough? Anyway, don't drink and drive. See—I'm not driving. Let this be a lesson to you.

1992

    Keys? Sure. They won't let me use it. You spin your own gold, though.

1994

    Hansel and Gretel—great show, clever escape. All I'd known was that other Humperdinck. "After the Lovin.'" Sorry, honey, I'm not ashamed to say I love those happy endings.

1997

Your Big Bad Boyfriend broke it off? Never fear, somewhere a handsome prince awaits!

2001

Have I been drinking? Lord, the left hand doesn't know what the right one's doing. Where was I? Yes, bride—you're a bleeping beauty! Go ahead: hate me, call me a sexist troll. Do you? Hate me? Can't hear a thing over this godawful gin.

2008

Happily Ever *Laughter*. Believe some party center beat me to it? I'm slipping. Anyway, just because you hardly call doesn't mean I shouldn't wish you many more!

2012

Honey, remember that old adage?: Into every life a little excruciating abdominal pain must fall.

2013

What's the one where the daughter doesn't care if Father lives or dies? When you get this message, let me know!

2013

Out of the Woods—there's a show I'd sell my first-born to see.

2014

    Docs are all cut and fry. Stick a fork in me, I'm done. Can't keep down a crumb.

2014

    She lost it? Honey, please . . . the curtain—that sun's no gold. Just a rotten apple seeping poison on my straw.

FIRST SESSION OF THE LAST FULL DAY OF THE LONELINESS SYMPOSIUM

The old man arrived late, lowering into a chair in back, hard-shelled suitcase by his side. Abruptly, before the last presenter began, he stood, squeezing the handle. "Sorry to interrupt," he said. "I can't stay—but before I go, just, well, marvelous job to all of you. I learned a lot in the time I've had." Hand to heart, the moderator said, "You are too kind!" The man paused at the door, tears streaming. The moderator stood, but he disappeared, the case following him out. I thought of a casket first, then hind legs, a dog eager for its reward.

MEME AND RESPONSE

What if everything you are going through prepares you for who you were meant to be?

What if Mother drank when she carried you? What if Father slammed her against the kitchen table, and she had to have you early? What if you nearly died? What if you were four, and Father started slipping into your room and said he'd kill you if you breathed a word? What if teachers said your attitude wasn't very ladylike? What if a funny boy gave you the time of day? What if he giggled you down to his daddy's workroom? What if, afraid, you lay there like a piece of wood? What if funny boy scowled, said, "Get rid of it"? What if Mother put you out with the trash? What if you kept it to make a point? What if you had no health care? What if they fired you when the register came up short? What if Lynn—your only friend—said I'll watch the kid for the night? What if, free for once, you just drove due south because you'd never been anywhere that hadn't made you freeze? What if you lay on the beach and when a boy stopped by your blanket you thought, Lord, not again? What if, while squeezing the wet condom into a napkin, he said, "I have a baby back home?" What if you woke in the Dreamcatcher Inn, turned on your phone, and saw thirty-three frantic messages from Lynn? What if you thumbed out your rage against the world and your little boy came on to type, i miss u bunch? What if—finally—you cried? What if you showered, slipped back into old clothes, and went home to work on the life you had? You didn't, of course. I'm just saying, What if?

HOW MANY WERE THERE?

At the wake, Luce admitted she'd splurged on a Read.

Jules winced. "Don't you think she—"

"Relax. This is the sub-basic package. It only tells you random ways a person spent their time. Did you know Mom spent fifty-seven hours and sixteen minutes of her life picking turkey from carcasses for Thanksgiving soups?"

Dad overheard. "When I die, do a Read for all the time I spent pumping gas."

Luce smiled. "For me, it'd be opening packages."

Jules said, "I'd like to remember Mom—"

Once, there was this jar of fancy Bolognese," Dad said, heaving into a chair. "Your mother was going to chuck it, and I said, 'Don't be dumb—we paid 5.95 for this crap!' I worked on the sucker until my palms turned red. She begged me to forget it, but I hauled ass back to that stupid store. 'You do it!' I told the manager. Two-three minutes he stands there twisting, straining—the full bathroom face!"

Luce laughed. "Did you get your money back?"

Near tears, Dad said, "Get this: the guy raises the jar above his head and smashes it on the floor!"

That night, sleepless, Jules downed a Dremexa—a secret, illicit splurge of her own. Darkness, stars, then Mom materialized at their old kitchen table, glasses off, studying a carcass. When Jules told Dad's story, Mom marshalled a smile and said, "Just one of the times he showed his love."

Jules recalled fists upon walls. She could still hear screams, shattered plates. Once, a blade scowled the air. "How many were there? The times?"

Mom spun the plate. "See what you can find on that side."

Jules obeyed, driving a nail into flesh that clung to bone. Above—between them both—the clock hands read aloud each dense second until dawn.

CREDIT CARD SONG

They'd played the one hit and the other one you sometimes hear if you listen to that station without commercials, but not the credit card song, the one our two hundred dollars a head demanded. When they said "Goodnight!" we laughed. Then the stage went dark, and we thought about the TV ad that faithfully played our unheard song, whatever it was called, with the rich falsetto that reduced us all to tears.

Now was not the time for tears but for unity. It started with the chanting—"Credit card, credit card!"—to show them we were real fans. Then some savvy somebody unsheathed his plastic. Soon, everyone was reaching for their wallets and purses. It was beautiful to see, the way the idea so quickly consumed us all. When we swiped cards through the air, they had no choice but to return.

"We'd like to try something new," the singer said.

We booed, voices high as interest rates.

"It's a slight departure."

We surged forward, arms raised in unison. A few down front gained purchase on the stage. Despite the chaos, you could hear quite clearly the delicious sound of plastic chopping down the air between us and them.

DEAR CROSSING

His son calls: "That way's no longer safe."

His daughter calls: "Don't make me take your keys."

For weeks now, the old man's been driving an old, neglected road that twists and turns like a snake surprised. Worse, the huge oaks that canopy long stretches rain limbs with every modest storm. Yet for all its peril, he's been finding comfort there.

That night, sleepless, he returns to the road. Poorly lit, curves unexpectedly appear. A sudden dip sets his stomach at sea. He taps brakes, flicks the brights. At this late hour, he's more alone than ever.

A brand-new hairpin brings him face-to-face with a figure on the road. He swerves then overcompensates, running into the ditch. He climbs out, head bloody from the blow against the wheel. Woozy, those lovely features still imprinted on his brain, the old man says, "Livvy? Love?" He staggers through tall grass, frantically shining his phone. Ahead—right there!—a flitting silhouette. No, several. Are those limbs? Arms? Eyeballs? Something beneath him snaps, and he falls on his face. There are voices now, indistinct, a party in a huge reception hall, and flashes of familiars he hasn't seen in years.

Late the next morning, the old man's son and daughter appear at the door. From his chair, he waves them in, where they stand, menacing in orange caps, Gor-Tex coats, and huge slick boots. There's the shotgun in his daughter's hands as well.

He adjusts the padding beneath his cast. "To what do I owe this—?"

"We were in the neighborhood," his daughter says.

His son adds, "Up the old road."

The daughter again: "A seasonal cull. Long overdue."

The old man cries silently at all that's hurtling back.

His son pats his shoulder. "Don't worry. Those trees are next. Then, halogen lights!"

THE GALLERY OF NEARLY EMPTY ROOMS

For each one gone, there's a room above that keeps it all for a time. But you're busy—just crushed—these days, so it's a while before you finally get up for a quick look around. You're alone—not that you expected a crowd. Images on the walls are moving but difficult to make out. That one—your favorite aunt. There, a childhood friend. Around the corner, hands on hips, Mom from 1985. You move closer, expecting words, a gesture, something she couldn't make when you kissed her goodbye. You're ready to place a hand upon her face when a buzzer sounds, and the guard admonishes you with furrowed brow.

Weeks of work drag by. A colleague broods about the "dull plod to the sod." Finally, a vacation gives you time to check back. The old rooms echo from near-emptiness, even as they remain burdened by the weight of what they'd displayed. Dejected, you move on, turn, circle, gape at various diminishments. A docent appears to provide an updated map. So much has been added since your last trip up. "The current exhibition runs until the 30th!" cries the flyer fixed to the entrance to a brand-new wing. Are you ready? Have you ever been?

Later, dreaming, whichever way you turn is this brief yet impossible quiz: 1) What were you expecting? 2) Why didn't you see? You wake, answerless, plagued by the knowledge that the space above has shown no end to its growing. In fact, this morning, construction appears to have intensified. You hear hammers and drills, feel in your chest the thud and whine and crash. Up, you don a shirt and pants. Dust twirls from a new crack in the ceiling. You escape to work, certain it's a matter of time before it all comes down.

SIGNALS

Missy found, through trial and error, a spot on the outcrop where she could catch a signal. Usually, it was weak, but if there was a breeze and she moved the device just so, she could hear her dead mother speak.

Today, a southwestern orientation, sixty-degree angle, yielded unprecedented results. "Butter, chips, vanilla," the voice said. "Preheat to 400."

"Mom?" Missy cried.

"Let cool for thirty minutes."

Missy called again. Static. "Damn." She spun dials. Shook the device.

"Anything?" This was a new guy, Leif, who'd been trying his luck on the mountain's northern side.

"I think she heard me!"

"Three weeks, every day. Nothing." Leif made a show of hurling his box off the cliff.

"Maybe your wife is elsewhere?"

"Most people from my sector have some luck here." Leif sat on a boulder and fished through his backpack. "I've been staying in a motel on the interstate."

He studied the sandwich he'd pulled out—a pale, flabby thing from which something brown had begun to weep. He took a bite. Wiped his eyes. Meanwhile, his device cried, "weeoohweeooherrrr."

The sound struck Missy as sad. "I'm sorry," she said.

"One more day." He chewed hard. "That's all I can afford."

Missy hugged the young man. While he cried, she studied the box she'd set aside. It was a pathetic little thing, with sensors thin as chicken legs. Reminded her of Mom sweeping flesh through batter. She closed her eyes, saw her family at the kitchen table. Strained to hear Mom's moving recitation of Grace.

"Hey," Leif yelled. "Watch out!"

There was mad tussle on the ground—wings flapping, box squawking. Missy dove, clutching feathers, digging in nails. She cried, "Oh no you don't!" as the huge hawk rose, beating hard with its burden toward a patch of transcendent blue.

A PARABLE FOR YOU KNOW WHO

Pipes burst in a basement, prompting a concerned neighbor to phone a plumber for the owner of the place. The plumber looked and said, "In my professional opinion, you need this fixed now." From above, the owner scowled. The gall of this man, thinking he knew more than what the owner felt. Those fancy tools weren't fooling a soul. The plumber, sensing anger, simply suggested he turn off the valve. The owner declared, "Don't tread on me!" Shrugging, the plumber left an estimate. Scoffing, the owner went to bed. Later, the water rose and carried him away in a rage.

BALL DROP

They'd yet to rebound after a trying year, but they'd made it here, two in a million at this bash on the square. For Jack, the crystal ball presaged better times. For Will? Well, he would just wait and see.

"Ten!" the crowd cried as the ball began to descend.

"Nine, eight . . ."

Strangely, the sphere was picking up speed.

"Wow," said Will, "it's really moving."

"Sixfive . . ."

Jack said, "Worrywort."

"Fourthreetwo ahhhhh!"

People shrieked and tried to flee the square. Will pushed Jack behind a dumpster as the ball struck, shaking the earth to its core. Windows shattered and chunks of asphalt spewed. Buildings cracked and crumbled. A handful of unfortunates were swept away by terrific gusts of a wind.

"We're alive!" Will cried, kissing Jack hard.

They stood, shakily, coughing in the haze. Around them stood scoops of rubble topped by sprinkles of confetti. It felt like summer now, a fact Will attributed to the huge crater that smoked and seared before them.

Jack stumbled through the haze, offering comfort where he could. "Happy New Year," he cried, starting to feel woozy.

Meanwhile, Will scratched his head before the crater, thinking, "Where'd the damn ball go?" He looked up and saw an eerie glow in the sky. It reminded him of the night they'd moved from the last of many neighborhoods, the threats having turned too specific. But this sky was different—the glow much more pronounced. It grew bigger, closer. Like that old messiah, this ball was coming again.

"Jack!" Will cried, running through rubble, past bodies in the throes of agony. He found his partner slumped against a broken wall, tiny squares of red and blue pasted to his forehead. Will gathered him up and ran, as if Away were a place that might gladly take them in.

SOCIETY RESPONDS HAPHAZARDLY TO ACCUSATIONS OF DYSTOPIA

- If you want to be politically correct, the term is "*differently topiaed*."
- Fact: No news is good news.
- Honestly? I thought we had a thing.
- Surveillance is the ultimate compliment.
- In the past, it's true terms like "food" and "water" had been too narrowly defined.
- We reiterate: only 1% of the infants have been subjected to the testing.
- We will never apologize for saying the trains run on time.
- This isn't a threat, but would you rather not even have an election?
- I haven't changed. Dude, *you've* changed.
- Are you still allowed to breathe? Very well, I rest my case.

THE CITY OF MY BIRTH

Under the city of my birth runs a rail line, for decades now unfinished. The tracks leap from beneath the tower on the square but break off near the lake, six feet of dirt before a solid brick wall. Lack of cash? Ambition? Available records will not say.

Over the city of my birth sprawls a lazy pewter cloud, also unfinished. It extends north and south and east and west before stopping cold for the blue beyond. No one will admit to building the cloud. A citizen once asked God, but he only deigned to drop his daily "no comment" card.

Beside the city of my birth is a second city, where everything shines with joy. You can see these leaping citizens from our crumbling viaduct. They're small from here, their features indistinct, but their giddiness is palpable. One might think they're making fun, but I'm old enough to know they don't even think ours is a place at which one might look.

Between the lines of the city of my birth is a long sliver that always burns. I pick and tweeze, cultivating a garden of deep red pain. Tell me, friends, could I stand it any other way?

LISTENAMERICA: AN EPIC FIVE-PART MINI-SERIES

Part I: Service to the Nation

Captain Mike strode the rows, saying, "You are not here to complain, correct, or critique."

Tugging at his starchy conscript duds, Todd felt exactly like a prisoner from medieval times.

"The purpose of this program is to LISTEN." Captain Mike stopped in front of a recruit to tweak his earlobe. "Absorb. Reflect. Understand where your privileged perspective comes up short."

The recruit, a skinny, sallow-faced man, drew fingers into his palms.

"But—and this goes against everything you've been taught as an American—you must keep your dang mouth closed!"

Greg elbowed Todd, grumbling, "Free speech."

Captain Mike turned, scanning the room for the guilty party. Fortunately, Todd had not yet begun to nod.

During the Country Overview that afternoon, Captain Bill asked, "Could somebody please show us where we're at?"

The first volunteer pointed with great confidence at the map.

"No, that would be the USA."

Twelve recruits failed before Nicole nailed it—more or less.

In the evening, recruits were forced to watch a long video in which these people talked about people they knew who'd been murdered by their own government. By rebel factions. Even neighbors. They had to listen about food shortages, diseases, infant mortality rates. Afterward, Greg said he thought it all was a bit much.

Captain Mike sighed. "Am I going to have trouble with you?"

Greg grinned. "Maybe?"

Days passed in similar fashion: grim historical context, graphic stories that defied credulity. Each night, Todd's bunkmate Pete declared LISTENAMERICA "totally unconstitutional."

During Week Two's Study Hall, Todd tried to draft his reflection. He wrote, "These people are . . ." Frustrated, he looked up, meeting Nicole's starry eyes. She winked and angled her screen, which read, "WE'RE #1!"

Up front, Captain Bill wrote "Facts matter" on the board. Todd nodded at Nicole. He even risked a smile.

Part II: The Real Eye-Opener

"You're ready," said Captain Mike, standing before recruits as they finished their morning slop.

"Ready to go home," Greg said.

Captain Mike made batting motions. "That's strike two."

"I speak the truth."

"Two and a half."

On the bus to town, Todd tried to sleep; however, his head kept bouncing against the window. Soon it grew light. Thick trees. Farmland. A hapless hamlet or two. Images of Nicole flitted through his brain until his stomach began to grumble. One of the many challenges of basic was not just bad food, but the lack of a mid-morning snack.

Eventually, they arrived and climbed out at a marker on the outskirts of town. Captain Mike introduced an old man. His name began with R before quickly devolving into a series of syllables and sounds impossible for Todd to follow. In halting English, the man told the story of civil war. Door-to-door butchery by people that victims had shared meals with only weeks before. Beyond them, beneath wildflowers, were bombs. A week ago, there'd been a terrific thud, a flash of light, parts of children raining down.

Nicole couldn't keep from saying, "Typical Third World—"

Captain Mike admonished her with a glare, which seemed uncalled for. Todd wished there were a way he could let this girl know how much he was on her side.

Later, at the barracks, Greg said he refused to believe Old Man R. Pete ran the word "propaganda" over his tongue. On her bunk across the way, Nicole asked, "Todd, what do you feel?"

He sat up, prickling, feeling very on the spot.

At that moment, Captain Bill burst in to say, "Don't talk. Listen. And get to bed!"

Lights out, Todd started a letter home in his head: "Dear Mom, Life is hard. Send more snacks."

Part III: No One Appreciates US

By the final week, the daily trips had become just another indignity to endure. Todd sat with Nicole and they chatted under their breaths, which struck him as sexy. He learned she was a fabulous soul. Raised money for the needy. Read to children in various urban areas. What might he do to impress her and, well, also make the world a better place?

Captain Mike shot up, hand on a seat to steady himself. "Listen," he said. "This is . . . the driver tells me we're approaching a checkpoint."

At that moment, the bus jolted to a stop. Captain Mike held on—he'd clearly done this kind of thing before. He said, "Papers, silence, and smiles."

The door hissed and two armed men in fatigues thumped on board. They spoke quickly—Todd thought: video game gunfire. When the man got to him, he surrendered his documents.

"The USA," the soldier said, handing them back. "Such violence. Forty thousand gun deaths a year. And you tell us how to live?"

Todd nodded. The solider mussed his hair and moved on.

At the debriefing, Captain Bill said, "That was a bit of unscheduled taste."

Greg, eyes rolling, asked, "Why does everybody always think we're the bad guys?"

Captains Bill and Mike looked at each other. Captain Bill said, "Well, back in the 1950s . . ."

The phrase "Back in [insert decade]" was one of many things Todd thought was wrong with the world. History—there was an awful lot of it. Who could even begin to know what was what?

Later, in the barracks, Greg said, "A teacher in high school said something I never forgot: 'Don't look back. Did Manifest Destiny ever once glance over its shoulder?'"

"That's the truth," said Pete.

Todd checked off his calendar. There were only two days until release!

Part IV: An Arduous Adjustment

Todd woke suddenly, bathed again in sweat. Since returning home, he'd had a recurring nightmare in which water suddenly went cold in the shower. There he stood, shampoo running down face and flanks, arms clamped against shivering ribs.

At the breakfast table, his mother moped. He stabbed at hardening eggs while glancing at an e-pamphlet he'd received from the TotalVictimsofAmerica (TVA). "Is Our Precedent Guilty of a War Crime?" the author wondered. At the bottom was a listing of chapter meetings—the closest forty miles away.

"May I borrow a car?"

"Yes," Mother cried. "Do be my sweet young boy again!"

He stopped at Greg's, who was sitting in briefs around a white mash of lightbulbs.

"Talk to me," Todd said.

Greg shook his head. It was bad—worse than last time. The program, Todd thought grimly, had done its job well. Pete, in contrast, was all energy but couldn't go because the video he was watching claimed the deep state was deeper than ever before.

Alone at the meeting, a gorgeous serendipity: Nicole, with teased hair and bold red lips.

"You survived reentry!" she said, stepping back after a hug.

"Not all wounds are visible."

They shared a moment of silence, each reflecting on the traumas they endured.

ListenJohn, the evening's speaker, took the podium. He was tall, skinny, with haphazard hair a flag bandana failed to control. "Elections have consequences," he began, arms wiggling.

Nicole whispered, "That's the hollow-faced dude from our platoon!"

Indeed it was.

"Don't feel confused," ListenJohn continued. "Feel used. LISTENAMERICA robbed you of your voice. Nothing less than our individual freedom hangs in the balance!"

People roared. Nicole squeezed. ListenJohn, although creepy about the eyes, made so much sense to Todd. For the first time since returning, he felt a spark of real purpose.

Part V: The Awesome Revolution

More meetings, more dates. Tongues and rubbings.

"Are you serious?" Nicole cooed, panties plinking to the floor.

"I'm serious," Todd said, entering her from behind.

Zealous sex proved their commitment to the cause. At the next rally, ListenJohn explained the LISTENAMERCA program was less service than sabotage, designed for no other purpose than to drag America's astounding name through the mud.

"Who's the real victim?" he shouted at the crowd.

"I am," cried everyone.

Todd had learned about other revolutions. The American Revolution—that was the #1 biggie. Later, the French did something wild as well. No huge fan of history, he nevertheless felt called to help preserve the original idea of this great nation of theirs.

A montage: more meetings and marches, signs and fists, picnics and mad love under the moon.

That April, LISTENAEMRICA veterans from all over pilgrimaged to the National Mall to protest. Todd and Nicole made the long trip, driven by love, by what they truly believed.

Captain Mike appeared. Todd and Nicole looked at each other then back at the man—his strained smile, the purple-black eye. He partially lifted his right arm, which happened to be in a sling. "I was wrong," he rasped. "Sorry for my disservice."

"Now 'Plug your ears!'" ListenJohn said, sparking a by-now familiar chant. The words worked like a current through the crowd. Todd and Nicole straightened, shouting the phrase, their lips a lovely inch apart.

ListenJohn closed his eyes, pleasured by the passion of the people.

Then—an awesome human chain. A million protesters or more, hand in hand in hand. Todd was warming up to history—the idea of going down in it. But first things first. Anger. Resolve. Elation at having bravely taken the first bold steps toward making a real difference in the world.

WE OPENED AND WE OPENED AND WE GORGED TO SAVE OUR LIVES

We opened things and ate them, one or two at first, savoring each morsel until they stormed in there and told us to get going, which we did to please them, shoveling and gobbling, more and more, teeth bearing down upon the things that ran hand-to-mouth faster than we could chew, and more and more we came to eat the things because they said otherwise you're going to die in it, chewing on and on, crumbs flying, a few of us stepping back to battle a choke before blistering taunts from one or more of them who moved now up and down the aisles saying faster faster, and we dug in deep with greater focus, to show them, even catching up with contents for a second, which angered them to the point where they said eat the packaging, wrappers and boxes, and the faster we worked the more elbows flew and noses bled smacking and chomping and tearing Lori calling out that Harry had broken a tooth and Kat mash spilling from her lips spat "truth—a broken truth!"—and as we inhaled more and more knocking heads and clawing arms we lost Kat not that we had time to stop and think what they might have done to her because there was more stuff coming cases and pallets and some after so long could not keep up so they crumpled under all that was still to go their cries quickly lost in all the crunching on and on until a cracking hard like bones or truth (not that anyone would say) and they really getting into it now started chanting come on come on come on, whipping hats at their behinds they cried, It's simple: when everything is consumed, all those voices you're not hearing will promptly go away.

MIRACLE WORKER

Drizzle, fog—it's not the most auspicious day. But as the wisps of mist disappear, there stands a pretty girl in a spangled top and skirt. Leg warmers. Ear muffs and cherry pie cheeks.

The tarp at midfield falls aside for a handsome man in stripes. Cheers. Horns and drums. A fight song frenzy.

As the soldier approaches, the girl's hands move over mouth and nose. The crowd explodes!

Closer, he doesn't look so hot. For one thing, the uniform's in shreds. Also—I'm sorry—there's considerable blood. It gives me great pain to state that he only has half a face.

The crowd groans. Some discernible boos. From the alumni section, someone yells, "Go back to Dover!" These people are upset; after all, they've paid money for a good, clean, wholesome show.

The cheerleader cries. The soldier shakes to his knee.

The coach of the red team says, "Fellas, a true warrior would never make a moment like this about politics."

The soldier teeters. He falls like a tree into the mud.

The crowd gasps. Thinking quickly, the announcer gets on the horn. Within seconds, four jets in a diamond appear in suddenly azure skies. Look!—see those spiffy whip cream trails? Everyone blinks, cheers, feeling holy and national anthemy.

The girl is screaming. Could it be the tragedy is only now sinking in? No, no—this is something different. Joy, fever, hysteria. She's jumping up and down, shoes spanking the back of her skirt.

For the soldier is now standing. Lord, he hath been healed! Plus (let's hear you sing-song it):

CRYS-tal's GETT-ing MARE-ied!

The announcer smiles. He leans back in the booth, a "my-work-is-done-here" smile upon his face. The crowd whoops it up. The soldier embraces the girl. All is right again in this unrivalled land.

ROUND AND ROUND WE GO

On the courthouse stairs, colorful signs bounced like buoys in the arms of old and young.

A man stopped at the light: "Why're you against them all?"

The organizer said, "Some are corrupt, some quietly complicit. Both are bad."

Three minutes later: "Don't you care about law and order?"

"We do. It's just we're tired of the law being out of order."

Again: "The officers have been charged. Why are you against them all?"

Round and round they went with him. Some, overcome with vertigo, sought relief in the shade beneath the scales. Those remaining cried: "Wetoldyouwetoldyouwetoldyou!"

Nevertheless, he persisted.

PRETTY LITTLE LAWN

The tailgate clangs. Three men stride with purpose across the street, teeth of their machines glistening like blood. Chewing a fat cigar, the boss says: "Howdy hey, pretty little green!"

Speechless, the blades begin to quiver. A pit bull whimpers. The mother across the street sweeps her child from the drive. On the corner lot, an old man pruning bushes slinks inside.

"See those windows behind you? Blinds down, central air hummin.' Shows your people ain't coming to the rescue. Fact is, they're the ones done put a contract out on your ass!"

Chortling, the men flip switches, rip cords. Explosions of noise. The pungent stink of gas.

Minutes later, an eerie quiet. The blades have been mercilessly mown. Wet, dumb lumps of grass abound.

"If this don't send the message now, me, Buck, and Slimmy Joe, we'll be back next week, bright and early, to cut you down to size again. Kapiche?" The man glances around, grin a slit beneath two body bag eyes. "Now come on boys, let's git."

Crash of tools, blam of doors. The splat of cigar on asphalt. Then the truck sneers off, righting hard at the corner into the blazing bullet hole of sun.

UNDER REVIEW

Whistles, three in quick succession, each less audible than the last. To his right, officials head for the hood. Above, the big screen shows a bang-bang play. No one, friend or foe, comes to lend a hand. The court becomes curiously aglow. The fans, in a frenzy moments before, are deathly quiet. No—there's no longer a crowd. The seats soar up into darkness, row by vacant row. This is a home game, right? He's home. The friendly confines of. The screen now shows a figure run through by the foul line on the floor.

Something huge has happened, which he strains to piece together. Feet moving into position. Hands up. The elbow. The blow. The snap and bounce of his head. Details swirl, but the hood grows larger, yawning, swallowing the officials. Banners, scoreboard, light—everything tumbles toward its maw. Someone, a voice barely more than a whisper, says they're going to a break.

A faint buzz. Voices. Laughter. The hood recedes. There's a blur of stripes at center court. A hole opening and closing, which becomes a mouth—his own mouth. He makes sounds. He croaks a "hello." Other words gather, like fans welcoming players off a plane.

"After review," says someone, "the call on the floor has been reversed."

He sits up. Pats his uniform. Squeezes his arms. In a snap, the seats fill in again. Chants and cheers resound. Music pulses.

Somebody fills a silent space by crying out: "Let's go!" A teammate pulls him to his feet.

He adjusts himself, wincing at a twinge in his chest. Sweat cools down his face. Another whistle. An inbounds pass. The ball thuds like a healthy heart down the court. After glancing over his shoulder at the clock, he reinserts his guard and slips back into the flow.

PASTWORD RESET

For the life of me, I could not remember what I'd created. Two Bs (maybe), a groan of vowels, one capital Y. Numbers—nines and naughts. Some unsightly combo of symbols—exclamation points, asterisks, a dagger of a dash. At signs, dollar signs. The dubious promise of an ampersand.

    I racked my brains to bring it back. Rattled every key. Years of "error" and "try again." Finally, a failure, I crossed fingers and surrendered securities to the machine. Soon, a message pinged. I opened it, welling up at my now and future code, convoluted as before, but beautiful because random.

SANCTUARY CITY

"I, David M. Lynch, as City Manager for the City of Newton Falls do hereby proclaim that Newton Falls shall be known as a Statue Sanctuary City welcoming statues rejected by other cities across the United States . . ."

—Newton Falls, Ohio, July 4, 2020

They marched down the path from north to south, merging at the base to cry, "Enough!" As a voice scowled aloud the story on the plaque, a terrible blow sounded against the statue's knees. Some clung to him. A woman, encouraged by shouts below, climbed up to wrench his westward arm. Then, looking him square in the eye, she shook a can and fired a swirling blast of white into his face. The woman gone, he began to rock back and forth. Ropes flew by his paint-bleary eyes. Someone spoke through a megaphone about the toxicity of myth.

An ungodly wrench from below. Screams. Then the pavement raced forward until it struck him full in the face. Howls and jeers. Screeches, sparks. He felt himself being born aloft. After reading a list of his crimes, they rolled him into the water. He spun through this silent, subaqueous world, thinking of long ago, the veil lifting for the first time, the governor declaring him "a truly great American hero."

In time he rose again, and was brought to rest in the park under a bright half moon.

There's a town for you," a goodly man whispered, toweling the statue's mangled face.

Brave souls placed him in a truck and covered him with tarps for protection. He spent a long, anxious time rattling in the dark, but the door finally slid up upon a beaming brand-new day. The goodly man wheeled him to a fancy gate. "Newton Falls," the sign announced. "Give us your tired, your poor, your huddled bronzes, yearning to breathe free." Before him rested a multitude of others—victims too of a war they could not fathom. With blissful eyes, the goodly man stood him up between Jackson and Lee, declaring all were "free at last" from further harm.

RESPONSES TO THE CHARGE THAT HISTORY WILL NOT BE KIND

1. Not very Christian now, is it? What ever happened to turning the other cheek?

2. Who? I've never even heard of the prick. Have you?

3. Oooh, I'm sure all the rotting bods will be shaking in their boots.

4. Eschew awareness. Be forever in the moment.

5. Well, my friend Future insists this is just another mad grab for relevancy.

6. Says the dude who's always running amok, for centuries on end. Why doesn't he just give it a rest?

7. His anger issues are well-documented. If you see him, here's a card for my therapist. Decent rates!

MONSTERS KEEP COMING

Now their nights are sleepless. And crowded. There's Embarrassment, a surprising and relentless beast, thin and slouchy, wet-faced and wincing. Those ping pong eyes, that diffident sheen. Anger shoves in as well, pummeling the heart toward the point of no return. Yet what a sick, hapless thing—bony knuckles, bloody teeth, loose skin from shameless burning in the sun. And, of course, there's crickety Grief, everywhere at once, too quick for the swipe of a hand.

Often, for a time, they find it helps to be on the move. Punch some channels. Skim a page in different chairs. She runs eyes out the window to the moon and back again. He sprints stairs to the bathroom. The monsters struggle to keep up. With the exception of Grief, they're such slow, bumbling things.

The couple keeps to themselves. No guests, no phone calls. Some evenings, they have a glass of wine in the garden. Maybe he'll mention the humidity. Maybe she'll remark on light through maple leaves. He doesn't know about her, but wine works for him. It keeps the monsters at bay.

One evening, he thinks: Could wretched luck one day lead to tenderness? They're genial, yet there's a stranger-like stiffness to their interactions. She wonders what it feels like to scream.

Before sleep, he opens an insurance email about "significant life events." Meanwhile, she changes into the tortoiseshell nightgown she's worn for weeks. In separate beds, their eyes drop over small dark print.

One afternoon, through the long thick fog of eventlessness, another monster approaches, huge and amorphous. Is it Truth? Or maybe Despair? Whatever the name, it stays in the doorway, beady eyes full of apology. "It's just," the creature explains, "I thought you'd like to know the death of your only son has made you rather boring."

BAD TIMING

My Late Mother

Again, I huffed over to Long and Pine, slapping up at noon on the dot. Again, she was nowhere to be found. I scanned sidewalks. Studied traffic. Leaned against a post with a poster that cried "Missing!" A beep turned me around. The horn, though, was no greeting but a "go!" to the hatchback dawdling under green.

Later, Lucky stopped by to say, "Come home with me."

There, I marveled at his family pictures: portraits jammed on mantel and end tables; school shots smattering walls; candids swirling under magnets on the fridge. Then these very people entered, back-slappingly alive. For dinner, turkey and all the fixings, stories smothered in a sauce of candied laughter.

At home, I wept to Guardian about my daily failures.

"No surprise," he said, ogling futures on a screen. "Chick'll be late for her own funeral."

A week after graduation came a miracle—a package from Mom wrapped in want ads and obituaries. Inside, an engraved pocket watch. Was this a sign she'd return when she saw fit? Maybe by Christmas. New Year's. Birth of my first or second. What if she were planning a big surprise? That, I allowed, would have to take some time.

My Early Father

Like clockwork, he was always there—but always long before. Therefore, I only knew him by the presence of what he left. "Sorry

I missed you," was the gist of those first notes, tacked to signposts or trees. Soon, though, the messages carried a sting: "No wonder they passed you over" was one. Another: "You know she's going to leave!"

I tried like mad to beat him there. Left at the crack of dawn and stayed until the sun died. Once, I spent the night. The next morning, a note teased: "Close, but no cigar."

Finally, I stuffed a pack with clothes. Raised a tent. By Friday, I was fired. By the end of the month, my wife was gone. Hair spiraled. Bones quaked. An incisor gave out. Sometimes, Lucky would stop by with a sandwich in a bag.

The last note—"You sorry-ass shit"—I placed with others in my pillow's damp sleeve. If all else failed, I'd read them backwards toward better days.

That Easter, Guardian showed to shake his head at me.

I yawned and crumbled crud from my eyes. "What time is it?"

"Early, late," he laughed. "Tell me why you think it makes a difference."

BAD APPLES

The barrel was some distance away, on the other side of the line, but even from where I stood, I could say with a great deal of confidence that it was filled with apples. I moved five feet closer. Yes, confirmed: apples. There were some Red Delicious, plenty of Empires, a Granny Smith or two. I turned to the others and said, "Apples. Good apples too. The best!"

Someone from the shade inquired, "How exactly do you know?"

I nudged my nose over the line. The apples on top certainly looked smooth and shiny. But in fairness, I may well have been assuming too much. I bent over more and saw one with a brown, thumb-shaped depression. Another had been gored by worms. A third resembled the face of a decrepit old man.

"A few bad apples," I announced.

"How do you know just a few?" asked someone else. "That's a pretty big barrel. What about all the apples underneath?"

"I'm not comfortable crossing that line."

"It's an arbitrary demarcation. And anyway, who made it?"

Up to this point, I'd been both patient and reasonable. Now, with these questions—these criticisms, really—I grew quite angry. Was I supposed to scrutinize every single apple? That seemed an awful lot of work.

"Where is the quality control?" they asked.

I shot back: "I wasn't even there when the container was filled."

"Why are you upset at us and not the contents of the barrel?"

I threw up my hands. They'd gone and spoiled it all now, these whiners gathered behind me. All we'd been trying to do is have another good old-fashioned apple festival. Why today is it so hard to have nice things?

Arrest them? Well, sure, if they continue in this radical vein, what other choice would we have?

WRONG SIDE OF HISTORY

Tickets went on sale at 10 am. Taney, seventh in line, had been camped out for days. Braved rain, sleet, jeers. Consumed power bars and Kool-Aid. Kept his waste in an insulated bag. When the gate opened, he bought six box seats and made some big quick cash on the four he didn't need.

At the arena, Billings devoured the view. "Awesome seats."

Taney smiled. "Those service fees, though."

"Seriously criminal."

"Can you say 'rank injustice'?"

They looked back. Attendance in the upper deck was pretty sparse. In the good seats, though—past the railing and down to the court—was a full-throated mob.

Billings chomped his dog.

"Good?" Taney asked.

Mouth full, he turned. "Better last time. Bread's stale. Meat's dried out."

"Look at these unpopped kernels," Taney said, angling the bucket toward his friend.

Billings swallowed. "But Jesus, these seats!"

"Next time, I'll be first in line. Going to be right down there. Behind the bench. When the camera pans, I'll shake my finger in the air."

"We're number one," Billings said.

"Got that right!"

"When's it start?" Billings asked.

Nearby, security swarmed. Bloodied, cuffed, a woman strained and screamed: "Can't you see we're nearly at the break?"

GRANDMA BREEN GETS CHRISTMAS MEAN

On Christmas Eve, Grandma Breen woke with one cookie-sweet conviction: she would wait no longer. Slipping robe over osteoporotic bones, she knew she wouldn't even ask. Again. Those days—and Lord, hadn't there'd been a shitload of them?—were over and D.O.N.E. done.

She moved stiffly down the stairs. At her writing desk, she removed the Rothko stationery and engraved fountain pen. She wrote about "Camp Oleander," two weeks of hike and splash along the fingertip of Florida. She wrote about the "Neverwades," the girls who wouldn't brave the water. "That's a good one, Granny. Right? Haw, haw!" She finished with "Love, Bree," thinking for the umpteenth time, "What a stupid ass name," her granddaughter a wedge of gooey cheese. But it wasn't the girl's fault—she hadn't come up with that winner herself. No, that had been her daughter-in-law's fine bit of genius, although her son—with his dumb acquiescence—was far from free of blame.

She composed other letters: a thank you for birthday money, a description of an art project, complete with her own attempt at hills and pines. Afterward, she licked the seals and stuck the stamps. She'd lost her license months ago, but that didn't keep her from the short straight shot to the post office. On the way home, she stopped for some Don Fernando.

Tomorrow, she'd send more letters, knowing they would faithfully return. When she died, the ingrates would find them tied up with a silver bow. Oh, on that day, to be a fly on the wall. A dog at their heels. A tiger clawing off—well, never mind.

Goodness—it had been a most productive morning! To celebrate, she brimmed her cup with tequila and placed three gingerbread people on her plate, where she could snap them as she pleased.

SERVING SUGGESTIONS

Early on, your father was, well, reserved. But one morning—goodness, I guess you're old enough to know—he came downstairs, jacket and tie, and saw a cereal box with a strawberry slit open upon a bed of toasty oats.

"Why?" he wondered.

I shrugged in my bedroom frills. "It looks nice?"

"Am I supposed to—?"

"It's a serving suggestion. Do what you want."

"If I just eat the oats as usual?"

"It's a free country."

His brows narrowed. He tapped his spoon against the picture on the box. "Enlarged . . . to show texture."

"That's right," I sighed, sliding a toe through the laces of his shoe.

Your father tightened his tie. "What this tells me is that there might, there might be more things that could be done. A whole strawberry, for example. Multiple strawberries."

I took his hand.

He reddened. "Perhaps some kind of fruity jumble."

I smiled. Let a strap drop from my shoulder.

"What?"

"I'm enjoying your train of thought."

"Heck,' he said, light flickering in his eyes, "Maybe—"

Coffee spewed as I straddled him. "Maybe," I breathed in his ear, "it's just time to rip that seal and shake some out into the bowl!"

SCALING THE NORTH FACE OF STUPIDITY

"Mon Dieu, the size. The appalling magnitude! It's impossible to get a true appreciation of it until you're there at the base."

Thrillerie looked back and forth over the bank of microphones. His eyes were red, cheeks dark with burn from freeze and sun.

"The North Face, although extremely treacherous, is the only possible route to the summit. From other sides, no human toe or finger could ever gain purchase. Our group started in early September, after waiting nearly four years for conditions to improve. We made it with considerable difficulty around the lower knob—what has been aptly referred to as The Chin. From there, what surprised us the most was the noise emanating from directly above. Deafening. Threatening in its utter incoherence. The high winds accompanying such babble didn't help. Not surprisingly, confusion reigned. We couldn't hear ourselves think."

He stopped to sip water. A sympathetic murmur bubbled up from the press.

"That's when we lost Jenkins and Kasongo . . ."

Silence descended. Thrillerie palmed his eyes.

"As you know, climbers by nature aren't conservative. However, at that point we had to face facts. Full of grief for our beloved comrades, we decided to turn back. The ascent proved too risky, with negligible reward."

A reporter stood to inquire: "Will you abandon your plans for good?"

"Jamais. We'll never give up." He took a deep breath. "For now, though, we'll be turning our attention to more manageable peaks in the range."

Later, from his hotel balcony, Thrillerie studied that sheer smug face as it glowed through the mist.

"Robert, je vais dormir," Dominique said, smiling around the sliding door.

"Une minute." He shook the cubes in his glass before drinking to his dead companions. Then, still smarting from the whiskey he downed, he went inside and climbed dumbly into bed.

THE DAY THAT'S COMING FOR YOU

calls at dawn to say they're on the way. Alarmed, you drop the phone. Shiver through a shower. Eyeball mirror fog, droplets ghostly punctuation upon your skin. You call family but cannot find the words. Again, the phone sounds: "Sorry, running late—have to make a quick stop." You text the friend who's always in the know. "Scammers?" he says. "Collections?" The phone buzzes again: "What are your favorite pizza toppings?"

Enough! You stuff a pillowcase self and drive due not where you are. Countless miles later, the scene's familiar, but in a sepia way. Another buzz. The Day That's Coming For You says, "See you soon!" You really step on it now, swishing and swerving until your cycle's in the gulch.

Broken, afraid, you set off on foot. Ahead, an uncut lawn. Beyond the arc of a sprinkler sits a pitcher of lemonade, a bike sprouting a banana seat. An action figure, hand raised, camps beneath a sprawling sycamore. If it weren't for strange yellow-browning at the edges of this world, you'd think you'd been here before.

Wind begins to tantrum. Striped shirts and racecar sheets snap upon a line. You pass under to the house. The door's locked, so you lift latticework below the porch and crawl beneath, letting the gate slap behind. It's dark. Quiet. Safe except for all the tiny pasts that scurry over your shoes. You draw back, hold breath until you can't. Smell seeps in—dirt and dirt before stronger scents of grease, cheese, meat.

A whistle and flash. The crack of twigs. Then a genial groan, otherworldly eyes beaming through the squares of the gate. Yes, yes, you've seen this all before—dimly, every single day of your life. "Time for dinner," the mouth announces. "And then, you naughty boy, it's lights out!"

NOT AS EASY AS IT SOUNDS

One night, I slap my pants and say, "Shoot, why don't I just go over there and change that stupid bugger's mind?" In the car, I refuse to kick myself for failing to think of it before. Because, you know, we all have blind spots. As I often tell my swirling minions, "What's life without some capacity for growth?"

He's sleeping, which is always preferable, although access can, as a result, become a challenge. But nothing here that a simple shirt-wrapped brick through a back door window can't resolve.

According to the literature, there's often a catch behind the ear; however, it's nearly always vestigial. I check first but come prepared to do some serious cutting. Precision is key. You're not, after all, handling a cantaloupe, although there will be times during the process when the parallels may be uncanny.

Then there's the internal debate about where to make the incision. And the size of it. I sift through my tool bag. Decisions, decisions. I'm loathe to recommend a specific saw—try a few and go with what feels natural.

Changing a mind is no walk in the park. Whatever you do, there will be blood. I've learned to bring enough towels to wipe and sop. Unfortunately, as is the case this evening, the brain is sometimes not where you'll expect it. Another round of incisions is required. Lower down. Behind.

Ah, there it is: miniscule, misshapen, flabby from disuse. I grab forceps. Twist and strain. Lord, it's really made itself at home in there!

Suddenly, a key at the door. Wife or child? Yes—Grandma too. I tie my tool bag, whirl it medievally over my head.

Some people say the effort's just not worth it. Have I mentioned the importance of ample towelage?

This is Norm DeGuerre, reporting.

STRIKING

Tell me: Does this piece move you? Is it "striking"? Do you feel it like a hatchet to your heart? Your soul? Is it striking a second time? A third? Is there blood now? Are you crying out? Is there a point in the encounter during which your head depends from a few threads of skin? Could you still be breathing? Are your nails scratching the ground in a feeble attempt at escape? Should I finish the deed now? And afterward, who cleans up? Or do I just leave you to stink under the calm exacting brilliance of my sun?

WANTHOLES

"The best way to explain it?" the specialist said, scratching his head. "You're a seriously bruised fruit. Maybe a road with many bridges out."

Mark was reminded of the stomach drop that stopped him when he read Cara's note, which she'd cruelly pinned to the zipper on his pants.

The specialist circled dark spots on the screen. "They're called 'wantholes.'

Cara had written: "I need more than satisfaction."

"Where's it hurt now?"

Mark thought, "Cara," placing fingers under his ribs.

"Okay. Now press."

He did. There was pain, but not more than before. Perhaps a good sign?

"See?" The specialist tapped the monitor. "That small area went dark."

He gulped. There was no way to deny the truth: He was caving in upon himself. "What's the cure?"

The specialist shrugged. "Stop wanting?"

*

Desperate, Mark decided to take the specialist's joke for daily regimen. He started small: tossing chocolate and chips, deleting numbers, killing dating apps. Over the following weeks, he weaned himself from rich food and sex. During rush hour, he practiced staying in the moment without sigh or curse. It was not easy. He experienced dark shifts in mood. Mortifying relapses. But each day was better, a little less filled with debilitating desire.

One morning, the specialist called: "I want to run more tests."

Cross-legged in the living room, Mark thought, "Physician, heal thy self!" But the line arrived to him feebly, like a bad joke he'd been told as a tween. Now, he was something else altogether—a being beyond irony and pettiness.

Later, he stood before the mirror, relishing his daily feel. Yes, he thought with hard-won objectivity, nearly all the wantholes had been filled with the steamy gravel of his indifference. Soon—three days?—he'd be ready to raise the truth about all humanity was missing.

WHAT A JOKE

So an officer, a guardsman, and a border protection official walk into a protest zone. The first guy has cuffs and a baton. The second fingers a tear gas gun, canisters shining like scrota from his belt. The third dude—he's the one with camo and shield and a rifle full of rubber bullets.

Protesters hold up signs. The three guys give things maybe four or five minutes, and then they just go to town. The first starts cracking arms and knees. The second fires gas at those two bitches over there. The third simply starts spraying, because when's that not a hoot?

And get this: they just keep on going. Crack, Wham, Boom. Oh, I forgot to mention, there are more enforcers behind them, marching together, shields up, visors down, striking out and firing here and there. Many protesters flee. Others crawl and writhe on the street, eyes burning, blood retching from skulls. The organizers—those commie bastards!—are seized and taken for a one-way ride.

Afterward, the third turns to the other two and goes, "*Now* let's walk into that goddamn bar!"

Ha!—get it? No? Come on, man! Ruins everything if I have to spell it out.

WANTED

Butch spied them from his window. White coats, needles, clipboards and file. When the buzzer sounded, he scrambled to the balcony. He tugged the bedsheet before climbing down, spats smack-smacking off brick. Next door, Parker yelped. He put finger to lips and ran, vest flying, bowler rolling across the lawn.

Behind, they shouted his name.

Butch leapt into his Mustang and took off, flashing lights in hot pursuit. He roared through reds, reared theatrically over tracks. Hard turn, slide, and CRASH! ("Sorry about that fruit stand, folks!").

Soon, the teeming city gave way to an inconclusive horizon. Butch skidded to a stop before a cliff's stark plunge. Behind, red lights scalpeled through clouds of dust. Damn, they were relentless! No choice but to leap. SPLASH! He swam wildly until the current did the work. Ashore, exhausted, he was surprised by a timely burro, which waddled him to town.

Where he donned a wig. Lost significant weight. And appetite. One evening, wheezing on a stool in a hotel bar, he noticed two white coats standing in the archway. One studied an x-ray, the other said, "We need another MRI."

Butch was gone—out the door and down to Costa Rica, where—a miracle? Universal health care?—body and mind improved.

But alas, nothing lasts. Lunching one day on the square, he heard disturbing reports. He dropped his fork, scrambled for cover.

"Come out," a voice megaphoned. "We want to discuss treatment options."

Perspiring against a dried-up well, Butch peeked at the square, weighing the cost of engagement. White coats eyed him from rooftops, from behind turned-over tables. Inevitably, the sky grew dark. When raindrops began to fall upon his head, Butch knew the jig was up. And to make matters worse, he hadn't even the strength to go out in style.

A DISVERBING PROCEDURE

Inspector B asked again: "Why did you asseverate?"

The boy scrutinized his nails.

"Is that a verb on The List?"

The boy was nonplussed. However, he didn't think it wise to apprise B of the fact.

"You have all been granted a reasonable range of actions to draw from. For this situation, let's see." B scrolled the screen before him. "Yes, you could have simply 'said.'"

Perhaps. But what would have been lost had the boy made such a concession? No, no—he was glad that he'd gone with his initial impulse. Asseverating had been most eye-opening, not to mention kick-ass fun.

"Look at me."

The boy complied.

"Do you know what this means?"

"Punishment?"

"There are rules. Guards!"

The boy was seized and dragged to the door. Was asked, "Do you have any last words?"

Mumbles.

"What's that?"

"Antagonize." The boy thrashed against the squeeze of restraints. "Bedevil."

A guard wrenched his arms.

"Cripple! Desecrate!"

Another struck him across the face.

"Dis-em-fucking-bowel!!"

B blanched at the boy's words as he was dragged away. With peace restored, he made a full report to his immediate Infinitives. Later, to unwind, he pumped his brand-new partner until it delivered that satisfactory ping.

TRUE STORY

A spring thunderstorm, strident but passing quickly. Typical Florida. Around recess, the sun began to dance, so Mr. Smith, seven-time Teacher of the Year, brought students outside. Smiled while they swung. Skipped rope. His knees buckled, though, when he spied Taylor Brights reading a book. Fortunately, it had been stamped HISTORY-FREE.

Alex Jolly began jabbing at the sky. "Rainbow, rainbow!" he cried.

Sure enough—two stunning rainbows! "Kids, kids!" Smith sang. Children pranced. Laughed. Held hands.

Next day, the principal informed Smith: "There have been complaints."

"But I've been so careful!"

"Rainbows. According to the charge, you told them to look."

Therefore, an emergency school board meeting was called.

In his defense, Smith said, "The rainbows were not stickers. Not flags. Just nature doing its lovely thing."

A concerned mother said, "They always say 'it's natural' when it's really a lifestyle choice that's all in-your-face."

A school board member said, "In fairness, according to reliable reports, the rainbows were not close to touching."

Jeers. An especially concerned mother countered, "That's just how they behave in public!"

"Boys must be boys," an extremely concerned mother cried. "And girls girls!"

Chaos ensued. Words fired in no coherent order: "Constitution," they shouted. "Bible," "Family," "Guns," and "Woke." Finally, the most concerned mother of all growled, "Groomer," which proved the coup de grace.

The vote was 8-1 to terminate. The board president explained, "The rainbows were there, but, like porn on a computer, it was morally irresponsible to apprise impressionable children of the fact."

The next day, a group of open-carry fathers crashed Smith's things against his door. On top of one box sat a bent monochrome card from the kids. Smith swallowed hard. Inside, it read, "learn" and "from" and "this." Except for a few signatures, all other words had been thoroughly redacted.

BIG THIRD THING

We were definitely outside. Above, a hawk soared. Beyond, the path burrowed into a verdant scrum of pines. And if there was any doubt—that sun! An hour in, I could feel its burn along the sliver of neck my hat failed to shade.

Blaine stopped to shake out gutsy hair. "Remember," she said, aware of my wavering. "Inside, Outside—eh. You, friend, are on the verge of the Big Third Thing."

"Not heaven?" I asked again.

"No. Just the *realest* real."

I nodded, squeezing water into my mouth. She was the expert.

After trees, we reached a bluff. There was not a cloud in sight. The valley zoomed down, a dazzle of saffron and green. Was this not beauty enough?

Blaine's eyes sizzled. "Here we are!"

"Where?"

"It's huge." She lifted a finger at the fat blue nothing before us. "Two of you'd fit."

I thought of Pat, once my "frequent other." His clunky camping gear. That mud-slathered ATV. Swirling beans over fire with a pocket knife. I wouldn't say he was a bore. I just knew I couldn't see him anymore.

"It'll close soon," Blaine said.

I thought to ask: "Why'd you come back?" but she was already behind the bushes, a titanium band across her eyes. When someone passed, she'd explained, there was always this brilliant flash. Heat too—and fire.

    I inched ahead. Pebbles slid. On the edge, my toes toasted.

    "A bit to the left."

    From beyond came a thunderclap and singe. A peeling sensation that pleasured me with pain. Further on, hovering, I experienced a blissful searing of eyes and ears. A melt of self along the curve of space and time. Blaine had mentioned an exit—a back door of sorts—but I poured forward, hell bent now on a blistering gorgeous more.

IN THE END, AREN'T EPIPHANIES THE BEST?

That first day of school, he realized aloud: "Each person is unique." Mrs. Freytag smiled, incredulous—that was to be her lesson for October!

When ten, a week before Grandma passed, he realized one should not take life for granted. Soon after, he realized what doesn't kill you makes you stronger. At high school graduation, while everyone cheered, he realized life would never be so easy again.

Word got out. In college, he became famous, something he'd seen a mile away. An interviewer asked, "Do you know you can't get everything you want?" The boy would have laughed, had he not long ago realized that pride preceded a fall.

Onwards, through those anxious, transitory twenties. So many ways he spared himself misery by understanding things in comfortable advance. He dodged drugs. Credit card debt. Ill-advised relationships due to pregnancy or sentimentality.

At his thirtieth birthday party, he was introduced to his future mate. Of course, he knew immediately she was The One, if only for the next phase of life.

At forty, he foresaw his child would not remain little forever.

At fifty, a concern: Had everything dawned on him?

"What's wrong?" his wife asked, keeping distance as he knew she would.

He might have said, "Don't know" if he hadn't realized only moments before the dangers of doubt. Still, a close call. He took comfort in a long-established insight—tomorrow was a bright new day.

Years later, alone in his garden, he looked up from the book he was finishing, stunned to realize how sad it was to have known all beforehand. He massaged his throat. Studied the plump shrubs that lined his yard. God, those febrile cries, the thundering apocalypse of hooves! Nothing, he understood way too late, could keep the enemy from thrashing through at every side.

CREDITS

"Quarantine" was originally published in *Ovunque Siamo* (Jul. 2020).

"The Height of Her Powers" was originally published in *FEED* (Jul. 2020).

"Last Days of May" was originally published in *Roi Fainéant* (Jul. 2022).

"Break Room, Smitty's on the Levee" was originally published in *Roi Fainéant* (Jul. 2022).

"The Ice Is Always Breaking" was originally published in *Ovunque Siamo* (Feb. 2021).

"Game Changer" was originally published in *The Wild Word* (Mar. 2022).

"Portion" was originally published in *Heart of Flesh Literary Journal* (May 2022).

"Conjugate" was shortlisted for *Flash Frontier*'s Micro Madness competition (Spring 2022). It was also translated into Spanish and included in the anthology *Instantáneas de Ficción* (Vol. 4).

"An Unfinished Prayer" was originally published in *Heart of Flesh* (Nov. 2020).

"The Wardrobe" was originally published in *Roi Fainéant* (Jul. 2022).

"Garbage Time" was originally published in *South Florida Poetry Journal* (Feb. 2022).

"They Will Let Him Know" was originally published in *Worthing Flash* (Aug. 2021).

"Misfit" was originally published in *Agape Review* (Dec. 2021).

"More a Nothing Than a Something" was originally published in *Third Wednesday Magazine* (May 2023).

"We Should Go" was originally published in *Ovunque Siamo* (Nov. 2022).

"Bull's Eye Is a Sign" was originally published in *Beliveau Review* (Jul.-Aug. 2021).

"Kimberly Maybe" was originally published in *Beliveau Review* (Jul.-Aug. 2021).

"August Afternoon, Delaware County, PA" was originally published in *The Journal of Compressed Creative Arts* (Oct. 2022).

"Long Light" was originally published in *Fictive Dream* (Feb. 2021).

"Last Dance" was originally published in *Microfiction Monday Magazine* (May 2022).

"The Angel of Death Victorious" was originally published in *Heart of Flesh Literary Journal* (May 2022).

"Way to Go" was originally published in *Fiction Kitchen Berlin* (Aug. 2020).

"The Arc of the Moral Universe" was originally published as "The Long Arc of History" in *Unlikely Stories Mark V* (Aug. 2020).

"First Session of the Last Full Day of the Loneliness Symposium" was originally published in *Dribble Drabble Review* (Apr. 2021).

"Meme and Response" was originally published in *Terror House Magazine* (Feb. 2022).

"How Many Were There?" was originally published as "How Many Were There? The Times?" in *Red Fern Review* (Aug. 2021).

"Credit Card Song" was originally published in a slightly longer form in *3:AM Magazine* (Nov. 2006).

"The Gallery of Nearly Empty Rooms" was originally published in *Book of Matches* (Winter 2021).

"A Parable for You Know Who" was originally published in *Sleet Magazine* (Winter 2020).

"Society Responds Haphazardly to Accusations of Dystopia" was originally published in *After the Pause* (Winter 2020).

"LISTENAMERICA: An Epic Five-Part Miniseries" was originally published in *Unlikely Stories Mark V* (Aug. 2022).

"We Opened and We Opened and We Gorged to Save Our Lives" was published originally in *Club Plum* (Oct. 2020).

"Miracle Worker" was originally published in *Sleet Magazine* (Winter 2020).

"Round and Round We Go" was originally published in *Unlikely Stories Mark V* (Aug. 2020)

"Pastword Reset" was originally published in *The Odd Magazine* (Aug. 2022).

"Monsters Keep Coming" was originally published in *The Wild Word* (Feb. 2021).

"Bad Timing" was originally published in *Uppagus* (July 2024).

"Bad Apples" was originally published in *Sleet Magazine* (Winter 2020).

"Wrong Side of History" was originally published in *Dark Winter* (Nov. 2022).

"Grandma Breen Gets Christmas Mean" was originally published in *Worthing Flash* (Dec. 2024).

"Scaling the North Face of Stupidity" was originally published in *The Odd Magazine* (Dec. 2020).

"The Day That's Coming for You" was originally published in *Dark Winter* (Nov. 2022).

"Not As Easy As It Sounds" was originally published in *Unlikely Stories Mark V* (Aug. 2020)

"Wanted" was originally published in *Worthing Flash* (Dec. 2023).

"True Story" was originally published in *Sleet Magazine* (Fall-Winter 2022-2023).

"In the End, Aren't Epiphanies the Best?" was originally published in *Cabinet of Heed* (Apr. 2021).

About MICHAEL COCCHIARALE

Michael Cocchiarale is Associate Professor of English and creative writing at Widener University (Chester, PA), where he teaches courses in American literature, fiction writing, and composition. He is the author of the novel *None of the Above* (Unsolicited, 2019) and two short story collections—*Here Is Ware* (Fomite, 2018) and *Still Time* (Fomite, 2012). He has also coedited collections of scholarly essays on the American short story, sports literature, and flash fiction.

About UNSOLICITED PRESS

Unsolicited Press is based out of Portland, Oregon and focuses on the works of the unsung and underrepresented. As a womxn–owned, all–volunteer small publisher that doesn't worry about profits as much as championing exceptional literature, we have the privilege of partnering with authors skirting the fringes of the lit world. We've worked with emerging and award–winning authors such as Sommer Schafer, Amy Shimshon–Santo, Brook Bhagat, Mari Matthias, and Amy Baskin. Learn more at unsolicitedpress.com. Find us on Twitter and Instagram at @UnsolicitedP.

www.ingramcontent.com/pod-product-compliance
Lightning Source LLC
LaVergne TN
LVHW092049060526
838201LV00047B/1302